'Do I take it you

Reece gave her a long ... unsure as to whether to ~~take her seriously.~~

'Of your motives—or of your methods?'

Slowly he reached behind so that his fingers brushed against her hair.

'Holly, I don't intend to cramp your style,' he said quietly. 'I'm fully aware you'd prefer not to have me around, but it won't be for long. Once I'm fairly sure of my patients, you'll be rid of me.'

He raised his eyebrows as he waited for her reply, but, feeling his fingers caught in her hair, Holly swallowed, unable to find words.

Carol Wood writes her medical romances based on personal experience, backed by her work in medical general practice. Married to a water-colour artist and with three of her children now living on the south coast, she enjoys conservation of wildlife, reading and curio shops.

Recent titles by the same author:

SOMETHING SPECIAL
PRESTON'S PRACTICE
PERFECT PARTNERS

A LITTLE
IMMEDIATE CARE

BY
CAROL WOOD

*First published in Great Britain 1998
Harlequin Mills & Boon Limited,
Eton House, 18-24 Paradise Road, Richmond, Surrey TW9 1SR*

© Carol Wood 1998

ISBN 0 263 81247 2

*Set in Times Roman 10 on 11½ pt.
03-9811-54593-D*

*Printed and bound in Norway
by AiT Trondheim AS, Trondheim*

CHAPTER ONE

DARTMOOR in October might not be every girl's dream of a glamorous weekend away, Holly told herself as she replaced the receiver of the staffroom pay phone, but the fresh air and exercise was just what she needed. Ever since Dr Peter's stroke six months ago she'd been working flat out—even her twenty-seventh birthday last month had passed almost uncelebrated. So, glamorous or not—

A sudden clearing of deep male vocal chords sent Holly twisting on her heel, her startled gaze falling on the senior partner's leather rocking chair, which should have been empty but was now occupied by two very long and unfamiliar jeans-clad legs.

'I shouldn't,' drawled the chair's male occupant, 'like to be in that young man's shoes should I have a puncture just as I was setting out for—where was it, this secret hideaway of yours—somewhere in the depths of deepest, darkest Dartmoor? Now, then, there's a scenario!' he jeered. 'One puncture, one particularly stubborn wheel-nut and one young man clearly in a fix. Does this master plan of yours allow for such an unpremeditated catastrophe, I wonder?'

Hardly able to believe what she'd just heard, but assuming she had heard him correctly, Holly stepped forward, her hands on her hips, narrowing her soft grey eyes. 'Excuse me, but do I take it you've been sitting there all this time, listening to my entire conversation?'

'Certainly not!' exclaimed the stranger, sounding as if it was he who should be offended and not her. 'I was sitting here, quietly drinking my coffee, when—whoosh! You propelled yourself through the door and launched yourself at the telephone like a whirling dervish. What did you expect me to do? Get up and introduce myself?'

'Well, at least you could have—'

Before she could continue he eased himself from the chair to a height which, even at Holly's five-eight, seemed neck-cricking, and with an expansive shrug of broad shoulders under a leather flying jacket casually sauntered past her to the door, wrapped four tanned fingers through the pelt of dishevelled, midnight-black hair and swept it back over the now deeply furrowed forehead. 'As it happens,' he muttered with vague irritation, though whether it was with her or the world in general Holly had no idea, 'I've an abominable case of jet lag so I think perhaps we should save further discussion—and any formal introductions—for another time, don't you?'

And, as quickly as he had appeared, he disappeared.

Completely confounded, Holly stared at the empty space. Master plan, indeed! Whirling dervish! Launching herself at the pay phone! The pay phone was, after all, a phone installed for the benefit of staff so what was she standing here for, defending her right to use it?

'Holly?' Tim Franklin, the youngest partner of Cancreel Practice, now stood in the vacated spot, gazing blankly at her. 'Are you all right? You look as though you've seen a ghost!'

'A ghost who was volatile enough to register complaints,' Holly spluttered, sinking into a chair. 'He—whoever *he* was—just sat there as cool as a cucumber in Dr Peter's chair and listened to every word I uttered, without saying a thing—at least, not until I put the phone down.'

Tim frowned, tilting his blond head to one side. 'Tell me, what did this ghost of yours happen to look like?'

Holly grimaced at the unpleasant recollection. 'Tallish,' she said dismissively, 'and darkish.'

'Oh,' said Tim despondently. 'Not much to go on, then.'

Which, of course, Holly realised, was absolutely untrue. Her description would fit seventy-five per cent of the male population of England, but certainly not him.

'Well, six-two or -three, perhaps. And quite broad,' she admitted, not able to meet Tim's curious gaze. 'Black hair and blue eyes—very blue.' The flash of colour in her mind made her shudder and, looking at Tim, she cleared her throat. 'He was dressed in jeans and an old kind of flying jacket. Somewhere in his mid-thirties, I suppose. And he did say something else, something about jet lag, I think.'

'Oh, heavens!' Tim gave his forehead a sharp slap with the palm of his hand. 'It's Reece! Damn it, I've missed him. I was supposed to be here to welcome him on Peter's behalf. You see, Marge is out on calls so Peter rang me from the hospital to say he's struggling through a particularly tiring physio session and would I do the honours if Reece arrived?'

'Reece—Reece Caine, you mean?' Holly was incredulous. 'But I thought he wasn't due for several weeks, maybe another month?'

'Change of plan, apparently.' Tim sat and poured himself a coffee from the ever simmering percolator. 'Goodness only knows, we can do with the help.' He gave Holly a rueful grin. 'So I take it you two didn't hit it off, then?'

With a wave of guilt Holly thought that if she'd known who it was she would have made an effort to welcome Peter's and Marge's younger brother, despite his attitude problem. 'He didn't actually give me time to say very much,' she complained. 'About three minutes flat!'

Tim chuckled. 'The man probably feels like nothing on earth at the moment. And the fact is, he's interrupted quite a career to come back to Cornwall. He's supposed to be top dog of an aeromedical evacuation team in one of America's sharpest accident outfits.'

Holly was well aware of Reece Caine's glowing repu-

tation as a flying doctor, but her esteem for the younger
Caine came nowhere close to the admiration she felt for
Peter—Reece's older brother by a decade. At forty-six
Peter had suffered a stroke and a subsequent gruelling pe-
riod of recuperation, through which Dr Marge and Tim
Franklin had soldiered on before Peter had hauled himself
bravely back to work.

'Oh, dear, I thought we were going to strike it lucky for
once,' Tim said with a sigh as Holly forbore to comment.
'I hope we're not going to hit any problems before we've
even started.'

'Of course not—it was nothing, just a misunderstanding.'
She tried to backtrack, knowing how much the return of
Reece meant to Peter and Marge—an event she would in
no way wish to jeopardise, especially by a few ill-chosen
words to Tim.

The young doctor nodded, looking more cheerful. 'Great.
Let's hope everything runs smoothly for the six months
Reece is here.' He gave her a long, meaningful look. 'For
Peter's sake, most of all.'

Holly knew Tim was right. The whole point of Reece
coming home was to take the weight from Peter's shoulders. But, as Tim was quick to point out, Reece had been
at the cutting edge of aeromedical work while general practice was at quite the other end of the spectrum. She just
hoped this unsettling start was not an indication of future
events.

'Cheer up.' Tim chuckled. 'Don't take your ghost too
seriously. After all, jet lag can make even mortals pretty
unsociable for a few days.' He took her elbow and steered
her towards the door. 'So off you go and enjoy your weekend, but don't get yourself lost on the moors!'

'No chance.' Holly laughed, but as she collected her
things from the cloakroom and closed the surgery door behind her the weekend with David began to loom oppres-

sively. What, she asked herself, did she expect from time spent in his company? Even if there was no romantic involvement—which, after Martin, was exactly what she wanted—their shared interests, such as hill climbing and country walking, had always seemed the ideal way to relax so why question her motives now?

Then another thought crossed her mind—a more disturbing one. Surely she hadn't allowed Reece Caine's sarcastic comments to affect her? Holly unlocked her red Fiesta and climbed in, determined to enjoy herself.

She would enjoy her weekend—she *would*!

Three days later—on a wet Monday morning—Holly walked miserably into surgery, nursing a heavy cold.

'Two paracetamol,' advised Alison, the practice nurse, when she saw Holly's streaming eyes, 'and home to bed.'

'Oh, no,' Holly sniffed as she dabbed them, 'I'm sure I'll be fine in a little while.'

'But will your patients?' Alison pointed out. 'Unless you're aiming for kill or cure results, I should let our new Dr Caine familiarise himself with your patients—he did mention something of the sort this morning anyway.'

'I'm sorry?' Holly frowned, laying her bag on the reception desk.

The receptionist shrugged. 'If I were you I wouldn't argue. Just go home and pamper yourself instead.'

'And since I can personally vouch for the fact you didn't plan for pneumonia,' said a voice from the doorway, 'I advise you do as Alison suggests and go home. You look worse than some of the patients in the waiting room.'

Holly turned to see Reece Caine, dressed in a smart dark suit, his hair combed sleekly back against his head, though the deep blue eyes were still filled with rueful amusement as he stepped forward, placed her bag back in her hands and, taking her elbow, steered her firmly into the hall.

'But, really, Dr Caine, all I have is a minor cold,' she protested, but he would hear none of it, manoeuvring her through the packed waiting room until they reached the surgery entrance.

'Don't worry, I'll see to your list of patients as soon as I've finished surgery,' he said as he opened the door, one long arm reaching above her head to hold it open. 'And it's Reece, by the way. Ah…Holly, isn't it, Holly Edmunds?'

She nodded, feeling an odd fluttering inside as he pronounced her name. 'Yes, yes, it is, but—'

'Go home and keep warm, Holly Edmunds,' he said with a chuckle, and with a final gentle push waved her on her way.

Holly defeatedly trudged past the pretty granite cottages bathed in October sunshine, admittedly with her legs feeling like jelly. A few early shoppers acknowledged her as they walked down the hill to the harbour where the fresh fish would soon be on sale. Unlocking the Fiesta, her reluctance to return home soon evaporated in the wake of a virulent sneeze, followed by a painful thudding at the back of her eyes.

Half a mile away was her warm and cosy terraced cottage. She had bought it two years ago when she had left Cumbria after her mother's remarriage and now the idea of retreating to it seemed suddenly alluring. Reinforcing Reece Caine's decision to send her home, she sneezed once more.

The journey took her only a few minutes, and the mirror in the hall told her she did, indeed, look worse than some of the patients. Even her resilient summer freckles had bleached away in the ferocity of that moorland rainstorm, the memory of which caused her to haul herself into the front room and sink with a sigh into the nearest chair.

She could still hear David's authoritative voice, insisting they continued their trek into mist and bog. Despite being dressed in all-weather gear, as David had persistently reminded her when she'd lagged behind, she'd got soaked to the skin. She had never really realised just how dedicated he was to all-weather exercise and how much she hated it!

Allowing her eyelids to flutter down, she decided to concentrate on something warmer. A vision of Reece Caine sprang, unbidden, to mind. As a surge of irrational heat went through her body she grumbled one last time at having been sent home before her eyelids closed like iron weights on her cheeks.

What seemed like a second later, but which must have been several hours, the front doorbell rang.

'Peace offering,' Reece Caine said as she reluctantly opened the front door. He handed her a brown paper bag filled with large green grapes. 'I couldn't square my conscience without calling in to see how you were,' he added swiftly. 'Also, I thought you might like to know I've seen Jonathan Avis. His mother rang in for a visit so I thought it was a good opportunity to make myself known.' He was now over the threshold, dripping onto the mat. 'May I come in, do you think?'

'Oh, yes...yes,' she faltered, and, gesturing to the row of pegs where her own coat hung, watched him slip the weatherproof jacket from his shoulders. Once relieved of it, he rubbed his hands together, gave her a bright smile and followed her into the front room.

Arranging the grapes in a bowl, she couldn't help but smile too. 'I don't promise not to give you my cold, though. It does, actually, seem to have got much worse.' She took another tissue from the box and tucked it in her sleeve for good measure.

'Oh, I'll take my chances,' he said cheerfully, sinking to the sofa with those long legs stretched out across the rug. 'I've been packed like a sardine into a crowded airport, forced to wait overnight because of bad weather and exposed to all sorts of bugs on a seven four seven for hours on end so I'm quite happy to gamble with nature, sitting here on your very comfortable sofa.' He paused, suddenly looking contrite. 'And, as you'll have guessed, I'm trying to make my apology for Friday. I hope it's accepted?'

'Well…' She hesitated, colour filling her cheeks as an apology was the last thing she'd expected. 'I suppose I could have waited until I got home, before ringing my friend…'

The black brows shot up. 'Not at all. That's what the phone's there for. I'm just sorry your weekend turned out to be such a disaster—'

'Shall we move on to Jonathan?' she interrupted as she sat opposite him, becoming increasingly aware that despite her cold she was breathing in the very distracting aroma of aftershave which had filled the small room.

He nodded, his smile fading. 'Ah, yes, Jonathan. I'm afraid I didn't get beyond a fairly superficial level of communication today. As a matter of fact, while I was there they were having trouble with that beast of a lifting hoist— surely they are entitled to something less battle-scarred?'

'I believe the hoist was borrowed from NHS stocks.' Holly sighed, inclined to agree. 'Did Gwen or Doug mention it?'

'No, they didn't.' He lifted his shoulders. 'But what would happen if the hoist really broke down? He's quite a weight, isn't he? And too heavy for his parents to lift at their ages. As with most disabled patients, mobility is a priority.'

The subject of Jonathan's condition was a sensitive issue for Gwen and Doug, who had occasionally resorted to lifting him themselves. Once or twice Doug had put his back out and over the past few months Holly had seen a marked deterioration in their health, although neither of them would admit it.

The problem was that they were devoted to Jonathan,

their only son. After his near fatal motorcycle accident eighteen months ago, when he had lapsed into a coma, they had kept a constant vigil at his bedside until one day, astonishing everyone, he had opened his eyes and regained consciousness.

'There will be no full recovery,' Reece said quietly. 'Jonathan will be permanently disabled, but from the way his parents were talking I received the impression they are hoping for a cure.'

'They've already seen one miracle,' Holly said after a few moments. 'Who can blame them for hoping for another?'

'False hope can be more cruel than hard truths.' Reece sighed and, catching her gaze, shrugged, then stood up and ambled across to the small bay window to peer out at the rain, obviously deep in thought.

His broad shoulders were curved at a graceful angle to his lean, athletic legs. The set of his head recalled the proud and sometimes stubborn streak which emanated from the Caines and made her heart quicken as, almost as if aware of her scrutiny, he turned around.

'You think I'm interfering, don't you?' he said, frowning deeply. 'You'd rather I just left everyone to get on in their own way.'

It was a rhetorical question, Holly realised, as everyone knew that Cancreel Practice had been running in its own inimitable style, perhaps not perfectly but, nevertheless, the Caines did have their own unique brand of general practice.

'Have you ever thought,' he persisted in a low tone, 'that one day Jonathan's going to ask himself why after three or four years he is still immobile? Why have the people he trusted allowed him to go on with an attitude of mind that can only ultimately bring unhappiness? What is he going to feel like then? And who will he hold responsible?'

'What are you suggesting?' she asked, suddenly alarmed.

'In all honesty, I feel Jonathan's case has been allowed to stagnate and the consequences will be dire for everyone.'

Hurt at what amounted to a serious criticism of her care of Jonathan, she stood to face him, her hands clenched. 'You don't know these people, Reece. They need to believe that Jonathan will walk again, despite knowing the clinical facts. It's what keeps them going and helps them to survive.'

'You're perfectly right—I don't know them,' he agreed in the same calm voice. 'However, I've an outsider's advantage. I can see the situation objectively and I'm fairly certain that very soon some kind of crisis will develop, although…' he shrugged heavily '…I may be wrong. I hope I am. Perhaps people can go on living in a fool's paradise.'

Holly secretly feared for the psychological welfare of the Avis family, had done for many months, but it had not been up to her to make the life-changing suggestions that a GP could. Instead, she had opted to support and do what little she could in the meantime. 'I can only suggest,' she replied, torn between her deep loyalties to both patient and doctors, 'that you arrange a practice meeting and talk to Peter, Marge, the health visitor, the physio and anyone else who is concerned with the family's management. I'm sure then you'll have a more overall view.'

He seemed on the verge of saying something more, but with an abrupt nod and a few words of thanks he walked to the door. She followed him into the hall and watched him slide his long arms into his jacket, wondering how much of a disappointment her answer had been to him for in her heart of hearts she knew the visit had been made to enlist her support.

'I'm sorry to have disturbed you,' he said and, turning up his collar, hurried through the teeming rain to his Volvo.

It was a parting shot which kept her awake that night as

she tossed and turned, wishing she had resisted opening the door to a caller who had done nothing to ease either the distress of her cold or her peace of mind.

Two weeks later, Holly returned to work.

The cold had matured into bronchitis and Marge had visited her, prescribing a five-day course of antibiotic. David had also visited, but on discovery of her condition agreed at once it was wise to motor back to the Lakes the same day.

This morning, Alison greeted her with, 'Hello, stranger!'

Bronwyn, from the word processor, added, 'Look who it isn't!'

In the office, Reece acknowledged her as if their last, strained conversation a fortnight ago had never happened. 'Good to have you back,' he said warmly. 'Are you feeling better?'

'Much, thanks.' She felt a little at a disadvantage. Marge had explained that Reece had taken many of her calls and, though unorthodox, he had insisted on doing so. 'I understand you've seen some of my patients,' she said, and hesitated. 'Thank you. I hope there were no disasters?'

'None at all.' He dismissed her query swiftly. 'Meeting them has proved the perfect learning ground. In fact, I'd like to follow up several cases with you. That is, if you've no objection?'

She guessed one of these would be Jonathan Avis, but as she was about to comment her gaze was attracted by the documents he held in his hand. She saw a memo in red felt-tip. 'May I be of any help in deciphering codes for you? That looks like the secretary's trade mark for urgent attention.'

He nodded. 'Yes—as it happens, blood results for Josie Dobson.'

'Josie? Our young sickle-cell patient? I thought Tim was

Josie's doctor?' The remark was made before she could stop herself, and she coloured deeply. It was common practice for any of the doctors to see Josie as almost everyone kept abreast of the child's condition and had, at one time or another, been called out to visit her. So her remark, although unintended, must have sounded as if she were hostile to his interest in the case.

'Tim is Josie's official doctor, yes,' Reece answered, before she could correct the mistake, 'but I thought it best to familiarise myself with her medical history. And, as it happens, we covered quite a bit of ground at the practice meeting last week.'

'Last week? Then I've missed it?'

He shrugged. 'Not to worry. It was a good idea of yours. I found it very helpful, especially since there were apparently other matters of urgency to be discussed. I'll update you as we go along, hopefully resolving any problems.' His smile was wry as he added, 'Should there be any to solve, of course.'

'But do you really think it's necessary for us to visit together?' she was prompted to ask. 'Surely this doubles your workload?'

'I think it only fair to Peter and Marge that I should have a comprehensive knowledge of what's going on in the practice. I feel if I'm to do the job, even if it's only for six months, I would like to do it properly.'

'Well, in that case,' Holly agreed resignedly, 'Josie is probably as good a place as any to begin. She is rather a unique little girl.'

'That's what I figured. She's starting a new school this term so, after talking with Mary Dobson, I had a word with the headmaster and school nurse to pave the way.' He paused, frowning, as for a moment he seemed distracted. Then his frown cleared and the deep blue eyes met hers with a powerful brightness. 'Oh, yes, I finally found a firm of specialist engineers to service Jonathan's hoist, and…the information I'd gleaned at the practice meeting certainly helped with my assessment. I had more of an overview on which to base my conclusions.'

'And,' prompted Holly curiously, 'what conclusion did you come to?'

He stood for a while, his features set thoughtfully, until at last he said quietly, 'In my opinion, Jonathan should be more active, both physically and mentally. His parents do everything for him and he is content to have it this way. I suspect this was the pattern of their existence before the accident. Jonathan lived at home and his stunt-riding offered only occasional employment, although, no doubt, he was dedicated to it. Gwen and Doug supported him financially and, to an extent, emotionally. After the accident, naturally their attitudes became more ingrained, their concern more intense.'

'Which is,' Holly added cautiously, 'corroborated by everyone you've spoken to?'

'Yes. But I feel, although Jonathan was severely injured in the accident, the major back damage is in the lower spine. There's no reason why he shouldn't, in the right frame of mind, set himself goals to become adept in a wheelchair. And almost everyone else agrees with me, too.'

The truth of it was, and they both knew it, it had been easier to allow the Avis family to go on in their own way. Reece was the first to challenge them. Holly knew to what extent Jonathan despised his wheelchair. Gwen and Doug had not quarrelled with Jonathan's refusal to use it. Holly had persuaded him to sit in it on the occasions she had visited, but she had always had the suspicion that after she left he would remove himself to an armchair or even his bed. The wheelchair, it appeared, symbolised a future Jonathan did not wish to accept but Reece, unlike everyone else, was not prepared to take the line of least resistance.

Reece glanced at her and smiled. 'One step at a time, yes? Leaving Jonathan for the moment, there's little Josie.' He turned his attention to the correspondence on the desk. The blue gaze swiftly assessed the paperwork, the sun-burned face and weatherworn features brought sharply into contrast under the thick cap of black hair.

'I was hoping we might see something of indication in the blood test. But the result doesn't show up anything we don't know already about her anaemia,' he went on thoughtfully. 'She had a mild infection last week and I treated her with antibiotic so may I suggest we make her our first call? After lunch?'

Holly nodded, unable to do much more in the wake of his insistence to power along in his own way. But surely she wasn't going to let his way of working intimidate her in a personal sense?

So, agreeing on a set time to meet him, she eventually took her leave, knowing his eyes missed nothing as she gathered her things and left the room.

Mary Dobson's expression lit up when she saw Reece.

Her small, even-featured face shone under her short brown hair. Her eyes travelled, eventually, to Holly. 'Holly…how are you? Dr Caine said you were off sick.'

'I'm fine now, thanks, Mary. It was just a cold.' Holly glanced at Reece but he was already bending to talk to Josie who lay on the sofa.

'Hi, Dr Caine.' Graham Dobson, a lean man in his mid-thirties, strode in with Joshua, their ten-year-old, hard on his heels.

It was a source of amazement to Holly how well the Dobsons coped with their adopted daughter's illness. Joshua, their own son, was asthmatic. The Dobsons lived for their children. Graham was a builder and Mary, unable to have more children of her own after Joshua, was content to be a full-time housewife and mum. The house was always a happy house despite their health problems.

Eight-year-old Josie's lustrous complexion was inherited from her African mother, who had never married Josie's English father and had given Josie into care when she was two. The Dobsons had adopted her a year later, aware of the frustrating illness with which they would have to contend.

'I've got poorly aches again,' Josie complained as Mary returned with a tray of coffee and chocolate biscuits. 'I can't go to my new school yet.'

'And I've got a wheeze,' said Joshua, not to be outdone. As fair as his little sister was dark, they made a beautiful picture together as they sat on the sofa.

'Double trouble, eh?' Reece grinned as he turned his attention to the boy.

'Coffee, Holly?' Mary took her aside to the dining table and poured a cup of coffee for the four adults. 'He's brilliant with the children,' she whispered. 'We've just changed schools and Dr Caine offered to talk to the headmaster and school nurse and explain Josie's problems.' She added quickly, 'Oh, Tim Franklin and the Caines are marvellous, but you don't like to ask for help too often because they're so busy.

'Anyway, Dr Caine was telling us about his life in America,' Mary went on. 'The kids were fascinated, especially by the helicopter work. The children see them flying over Cancreel but they've never actually met someone who flies in them. He really has a way with him, doesn't he?'

It was clear Reece loved children. He had a natural ease about him to which they responded and which was demonstrated as a burst of laughter came from the sofa.

'Both chests clear—as you can hear,' he told Mary. 'The antibiotic has helped Josie's breathing, but I'm going to prescribe some analgesics for her "poorly aches".' He turned back to ruffle Josie's ebony hair and Holly watched him with the children as he talked quietly and told them jokes, finally glancing back to Mary who merely lifted her brows.

'Well, let us know how Josie is over the next few days, won't you?' Reece said as he got up, stretching his long legs and winking at the little girl as he left.

It wasn't until after the visit when they sat in the blue Volvo, borrowed from Peter, that Holly momentarily forgot about the Dobsons as, on a more personal note, she wondered if it had been wise to agree to travel together. Despite trying to concentrate on her notes, her gaze wandered, as it had so frequently before, to the strong hand clamped firmly around the mobile and the brown wrist emerging from the coat cuff. A solid watch was strapped to it, the gold trim glinting as he moved. The green cloth of his coat brushed against the dark, hair-strewn skin.

'Josie's a lovely kid,' he said, startling her from her reverie. 'Mary and Graham seem to be able to manage the sickle cell—not an easy job, by any means.'

Holly nodded, knowing all too well the unpredictable illness was a constant worry for the Dobsons; the Haemoglobin S or premature destruction of red cells to become deformed in shape in parts of the body where the person's oxygen was low was a genetic disease passed on from Josie's African birth parents.

'You seem to have captured their imaginations,' she remarked on a lighter note, thinking the Dobson's were not the only ones to be impressed. 'Mary tells me the children were fascinated by your helicopter stories.'

He laughed. 'Oh, those! It helps to build up a bit of a rapport, that's all. Especially with kids. You need some kind of devise to win their trust.'

'And is that your philosophy with grown-ups too?'

He gave her a long, searching look as though unsure as

to whether to take her seriously. 'Do I take it you don't approve?'

'Of your motives—or of your methods?'

Slowly he reached behind to place his hand on the back of the seat so that his fingers brushed against her hair. 'Holly, I don't intend to cramp your style, you know,' he said quietly, 'and I'm fully aware you'd prefer not having to haul around with me, but it won't be for too long. Once I'm fairly sure of my patients, you'll be rid of me.' He raised his eyebrows as he waited for her reply, but, feeling the light twist of her hair spin down to her scalp as his fingers accidentally caught in the silky strands, she swallowed, unable to find words.

Taking her silence for confirmation, he shrugged slightly and, as if setting her free from the spell, brought his arm down, reached out for the steering wheel and with his other hand turned the key in the ignition. The burst of life which followed seemed to coincide with the racing of her heart as she instructed her eyes back to the road and her breath to expel fully from her tightly constricted lungs.

CHAPTER TWO

REECE drove along the narrow lanes, interweaving the cliff-top, and Holly caught her breath at the first sight of the rugged Cornish coastline, a view that never ceased to enthral her.

It seemed almost impossible that a few miles on, as they turned southward and away from the sea, the windswept, craggy vista would melt into countryside and reveal the sudden and surprising sight of a small housing estate perched on the gentle slope of a hill. Here was Jonathan's parents' bungalow and Gwen Avis, a small woman in her late fifties, welcomed them, leading them directly along the hall and into Jonathan's bedroom.

'Hi, Holly, Dr Caine,' Jonathan called from his bed, looking up from the magazine he was reading.

'A Harley?' Reece nodded to the glossy photograph of the motorbike on its front cover and whistled through his teeth. 'Some machine.'

'Best bikes in the world,' agreed Jonathan enthusiastically.

'Personally, I'd settle for something a little less spirited,' Reece observed with a wry smile. 'Like a Norton?'

Jonathan's gaunt face and high cheek-bones showed sudden animation under his light brown hair. 'Brilliant bikes! Have you ridden one?'

'Oh, one or two when I was in my teens.' As Reece sat on the chair beside Jonathan's bed Gwen drew Holly outside and the two women walked to the bathroom, talking of what had happened since Holly's last call. 'Dr Caine had the hoist engineers here within the day,' Gwen explained

22

gratefully, 'and they seem to have put the mechanism right.'

In the bathroom Holly placed her bag on the cabinet and spread its contents over the little table. 'In which case, would you like me to give Jonathan a bath today?' Holly suggested. 'Then we could make him comfortable in his chair and perhaps push him into the conservatory for a few minutes.'

'Oh, no,' Gwen said quickly. 'Doug and I gave him his wash early this morning and it's a wee bit chilly for him to go into the conservatory.' She hesitated, glancing at Holly from the corner of her eye. 'There's some talk from the engineers about the hoist needing to be replaced—has Dr Caine mentioned it to you?'

'I can't say I'm surprised,' Holly admitted. 'This one was originally only on loan, wasn't it?'

'But now it's fixed I'm sure we'll manage,' the older woman said brightly. 'To be honest, we couldn't possibly afford a new hoist.'

Holly nodded, aware that Gwen's and Doug's small income from their life savings had been whittled away in their efforts to keep the family afloat. Knowing that the subject of finance was always a sensitive one for Gwen, Holly steered the conversation to more mundane matters. 'I expect you'll be needing some incontinence drainage bags and Sudocrem for bed sores—how are you fixed, Gwen?'

'Oh, yes, I do,' Gwen agreed, and Holly kept up the easy flow of chatter as they sorted through the various items for Jonathan. When finally they had completed their small inventory and replenished supplies they rejoined the men to discover Jonathan in high spirits.

'Well, come on, what's the joke?' Gwen manoeuvred her son into a better sitting position, pushing pillows firmly behind his back.

'Not for ladies' ears.' Doug chuckled, having come in from his chores in the garden.

'These are the nineties,' exclaimed Gwen, poking her husband in the ribs. 'Or haven't you noticed?'

Holly laughed, aware that humour was one of the things which helped to alleviate the trauma the family had faced since the nightmare day, eighteen months ago, when Jonathan had crashed his motorbike during the performance of a speedway stunt. Though Gary Sharpe, Jonathan's co-rider, had survived relatively intact, Jonathan had sustained irrevocable spine damage and had lain in a coma for three months, before making a remarkable and unexpected recovery.

However, apart from spasmodic visits to the day centre, which Jonathan did not much care for, both parents now looked after Jonathan full time. Though humour had sustained them so far, Holly now sensed the tension which lay just beneath the surface.

'Is Gary in the magazine this month?' Holly asked, referring to the new issue of *Speed Monthly*. Gary Sharpe had continued his speedway riding and visited Jonathan frequently in order to pass on the news of his latest exhibition of stunt-riding.

'Main feature,' said Jonathan. 'He's the greatest.'

'Look, here it is.' Doug pulled the magazine across the bed and proudly displayed the centre feature.

Reece acknowledged the article, then turned his attention back to Jonathan, frowning slightly. 'I'd like to see you having extra physio and coming into the day centre more frequently, Jonathan, but we'll have a chat about that on my next visit.'

Jonathan was silent and Holly realised it was a subject Reece must have tried to broach before and which had met with a cool reception. 'See you next week, then,' Reece said, and left Jonathan, reading his magazine.

In the hall Reece did not speak immediately but then he glanced at Gwen. 'I'm going to raise your son's fluid intake to 2000 ml daily, Mrs Avis. I don't want another urinary tract infection starting so it's very important he drinks as much as he can.'

'He's a devil at taking his drink,' admitted Gwen, as though Jonathan were a six-year-old. 'I have to fairly tip it down him.'

Reece was, again, silent. Then, raising his brows, he nodded to the wheelchair placed redundantly under the stairs. 'The hoist is working well enough now. Perhaps this would be an appropriate time to persuade him to spend a few more hours each week at the day centre.'

But Gwen's face clouded. 'Well…it's not that we're ungrateful for all you've done, Dr Caine, but since Jonathan's accident he's never lost hope of a full recovery, despite what the doctors have told him. They maintain his legs will be permanently paralysed but, then, they also said in hospital he might never regain consciousness. Since then his father and I take each day as a bonus, and if the day centre depresses Jonathan then, in our view, it's the wrong place for him to be.'

'I understand,' said Reece sympathetically, 'but, as a young man, he needs to socialise with other people and you also need some time to yourselves.'

'Oh, we're all right,' responded Gwen briskly. 'And Jonathan has plenty of feedback from the speedway circuit—Gary never fails to make him still feel part of the team.'

Reece gave Holly a brief glance and then led the way to the front door. After saying goodbye to Gwen, they climbed into the Volvo and Reece rubbed his chin thoughtfully. 'You know, I'm not happy about the situation here. Not happy at all.'

'Well, I agree it's not ideal.' Holly sighed. 'But it has to be said that Jonathan is content to still be part of the racing circuit, keeping up with all the news from Gary.'

Reece turned to frown at her. 'I understand from Gwen he's always brushed the paralysis to one side—and so have they, come to that. Fine, if it's with an attitude of acceptance, not denial. By now they should be thinking towards a higher standard of independence—with the paralysis as a permanent factor in their lives, not something that will just disappear one day.'

'I wouldn't go so far as to say they hope it will disappear,' Holly found herself arguing. 'I think they feel he has done so well that, after almost losing him, they are willing to compromise—for the time being.'

As he made no response she decided to ask whom he had in mind to visit next but the mobile shrilled and he answered it, his dark brows knitting in a frown of concentration as he listened.

Holly was thankful for the momentary respite, reflecting how rare it was to argue a point with Peter who took such a different attitude to his patients. The elder brother, who had attended Jonathan since his accident, had managed the case with sympathy and understanding, but whereas Peter had allowed the healing to take its own natural course Reece showed every sign of wanting to speed up the process.

Perhaps because Peter himself had been ill, things had been allowed to drift a little and Marge had not intervened, accepting Peter's judgement on the case despite spasmodic attempts to encourage visits to the day centre.

Holly was sympathetic to Marge's position, aware the doctor had suffered much personal trauma, having lost her husband to cancer five years ago and then, after moving back to Chartwell House, the family home, she'd been faced with Peter's unexpected stroke. Fortunately, the practice had managed to keep going despite the setbacks.

Though its cohesive family atmosphere was well appreciated by its patients, locums had not welcomed the pressures involved with such a large and isolated catchment area.

Holly found herself staring at the firm, wide mouth talking into the mobile and the deep blue eyes flashing alertly through the windscreen. Just for one moment, as he moved, she was aware of the smooth graininess of his tanned skin and the dark beard, already threatening to form on the clean outline of his jaw. The sensation it gave her shocked her, bringing a warm flush into her cheeks.

As though aware of her scrutiny, he suddenly turned and she lowered her eyes, raising her hand to mask her face—drawing her fingers through her dark hair to loop it behind her ear.

'Panic's on at the practice,' he told her, laying the mobile on the back seat. 'We had better get back.' His eyes dragged briefly over her face and then, starting the car, to her great relief, he returned his attention to the road.

At the surgery they parted company. Holly returned to the Fiesta and paused to reflect, not allowing herself to analyse her personal reaction towards Reece but to consider the problem of Jonathan's management. His remarks made her examine her methods and motives. Was she too close to her patients, too protective, too apathetic or too loyal to Peter and Marge—or, worse, was she being cowardly and inflexible?

Unable to ease her mind, she started up the car and decided to follow her own advice to her patients—to try to adapt to new circumstances, Reece's own unparalleled style not the least of them.

By the end of the week, Holly knew Peter and Marge were feeling the pressure, too.

At Reece's insistence they had taken on a new receptionist and Bronwyn had been fully occupied with her training. Peter had seemed distant on several occasions and Marge, who was usually chatty and easygoing, had been preoccupied, too. Friday was usually reserved for clinics. Alison ran a heart-check day and the antenatals came at teatime to see Marge and then were weighed and BPs taken by Alison. So it was usually busy.

But when Holly arrived in the morning Peter called her into his room. He was looking tired and he rubbed his arm as if to bring back the blood supply, a habit he had acquired post-stroke.

'Alison's not in,' he told her wearily. 'Her youngest has chickenpox. Obviously in the early stages of the virus, she doesn't want to come into contact with pregnant mothers. I'm afraid we're going to be very short staffed nursing-wise.'

It took only a few seconds for Holly to realise what Peter was driving at. 'I'll fill in for Alison, if you wish,' she offered without hesitation. 'I've only two visits necessary for today. The others I can catch up on in my own time.'

Peter breathed a sigh of relief. 'That would be wonderful, Holly. And perhaps Reece can help out by visiting your two patients. It does make sense, actually, as he's on call.'

Holly began to protest but Peter was already turning away. Feeling any objection on her part might arouse his concern, she did not press the point. She watched him move slowly into his consulting room, his fair, thinning hair dishevelled over his collar. Though very little evidence remained of his facial stroke damage, today she noticed the laboured inflections had returned to his voice.

At that moment she heard a small bump, followed by a soft groan, and Holly hurried after him, only to discover he had collided with the desk and knocked a number of records to the floor.

'I'm fine, I'm fine,' he told her as she reached out to

help him. 'I'm so darned awkward. I seem to get myself in such a mess these days.'

'Oh, rubbish.' Holly smiled, making light of it. 'Back at work after only six months' rest—you've amazed us all.'

He sat down heavily in his swivel chair, and as it threatened to skid on the floor Holly put out a hand to steady it.

He gave her a rueful smile. 'Thanks. Whatever should I do without my wonderful staff?' Bringing together his brows, he glanced up at her. 'Are you really sure you're happy to stand in for Alison?'

'Of course.' Holly reassured him. 'I'll pop out to Bronwyn and explain.' She put a hand on his shoulder. 'Sit where you are and I'll get her to bring you in a coffee, too.'

'Thanks, Holly. You're a good girl.' He lifted his hand and cupped hers, giving it a grateful squeeze. At just that moment, startling them both, Reece appeared. His gaze went immediately to their linked hands and Holly drew away her hand more sharply than she'd intended.

Peter attempted to do the same, but he was slower and made the break look clumsy. 'Oh, Reece, you're here. Good man,' he said over-brightly.

Holly took a breath in order to regain her composure, though she was annoyed with herself for losing it over something so small.

'I think you'll be seeing two of my patients today,' she ventured, addressing Reece, 'so would you call in to Alison's room before you leave, by which time I'll have their notes ready?' She looked back at Peter and smiled. 'Don't worry, we'll sort everyone out.'

Peter returned her smile and Holly made her exit, avoiding Reece's gaze. Once in Reception she explained to Bronwyn the new pattern the day would take. In Alison's room she began to prepare the trolley and set out fresh equipment for the ear-syringing and the sphygmomanometer for BPs. She then lifted her case to the desk and took out her notes, trying to refocus her disturbed concentration.

Why she should feel so disturbed she had no idea. Perhaps it had been something in Reece's judgmental stare which had caught her off balance. When the tap came on the door and Reece entered she almost physically jumped.

'Who is it you would like me to see?' he asked at once.

'If you're sure it's no trouble,' she began hesitantly, 'it was actually your brother's suggestion—I'm perfectly prepared to go after clinic.'

'Not necessary,' he said, shrugging and picking up the two folders on her desk. 'Are these your notes?'

She nodded. 'I've seen Mr Bevan once before. He's a forty-year-old patient of Peter's, discharged this week from hospital after an inguinal hernia repair. He's worrying about getting back to work, but I tried to persuade him that a hernia in the lower abdomen will take time—especially in his trade, where the injury was initially sustained. He has to lift crates and furniture as a removals contractor—'

'I think I'll be able to digest the written word,' Reece interrupted her coolly. When she looked at him with surprise she found him staring at her in a strange way. 'I must have interrupted you and Peter just now,' he said.

She frowned. 'Not at all. We were just—'

As she was about to explain Peter's minor accident Bronwyn knocked and, without pausing, poked her head around the open door. 'There's a pregnant mum in the waiting room, Dr Caine. She thinks she might be starting labour. Can you come?'

'I'll be along directly. My room's free—take her in.' He glanced back to Holly as Bronwyn disappeared. 'Is there anything else I should know, regarding your patients—anything not written on the notes?'

Holly shrugged. 'I don't think so. The other man is a seventy-one-year-old retired seaman. Ben Sharman is cared for by home-care workers and the odd neighbour and he's just had a catheter fitted in hospital, which is giving him a problem.'

'Have we a male nurse to contact, should the need arise?'

'No…no.' Her surprise registered in her voice. 'Up until now I've been calling on him. I'm quite sure he won't have any objections. Why should he?'

Reece lifted an eyebrow. 'Oh, nothing, except that some men do prefer to see a male nurse for this kind of thing, just as women often prefer female doctors or nurses for procedures such as smears. Anyway, I'll not press the point if all is well. And I'd better see this pregnant lady.' Leaving her to stare after him, he left the room.

Ben Sharman had always been content to have her call on him, although it was the first time he had been fitted with a catheter. She hadn't given a thought to the fact he might prefer a male nurse. However, she was sure that, once over the initial small problems a catheter might present, they would iron out any embarrassment the appliance might cause.

Resolving to put aside her worries—maybe she was altogether too sensitive where Reece was concerned—she tried to settle down to the morning's clinic. Her first patient, an elderly lady who unravelled her stocking to reveal the dressings Alison had applied to her leg ulcer, talked away cheerfully as Holly cleaned and bathed the broken skin. When fresh dressings had been applied and the stocking pulled up, she went on her way, leaving Holly to see the next patient sent in by Peter.

The man had trapped something in his eye whilst operating a crane on the sea-front. Although there was no discernible debris in the eye, avoiding the cornea, Holly applied the preparation Peter had suggested. Soon the healing ointment was gently absorbed into the conjunctival sac and the labourer gratefully accepted a temporary patch which he could use while at work.

After two more patients for ear-syringing Marge appeared, pausing briefly in the doorway. 'Have you eaten lunch yet?' Her light brown hair and hazel eyes were the same shade and had the same soft expression as Peter's, Holly noted—so in contrast to Reece's vivid blue gaze.

'Not yet,' Holly admitted, blinking away the recollection of Reece's earlier unsettling visit. 'I was just going to the local café for a sandwich.'

'Well, join me in the staffroom, if you've an appetite,' Marge suggested amiably. 'I've some home-made quiche and potato salad that needs eating up. Peter and Reece flatly refuse to confront any more.'

Holly laughed. 'Only because they're too well fed. You spoil them, Marge.'

'Yes, for my sins, I do.' Marge grinned. 'See you soon.'

Holly tidied her room, grateful Marge had thought of her. Consideration to the staff was one of the older woman's most attractive qualities. She was never too busy to remember them and always made sure the staffroom was provided with coffee, a good Ceylon tea and cookies.

When Holly arrived upstairs Marge was standing at the refreshment bar, had already portioned off the mushroom quiche and was about to add salad.

'I'll have to loosen my belt,' Holly joked as she pressed her blue uniform over her flat stomach. Taking several knives and forks and two paper serviettes from the drawer, she set them on the oval table. 'It looks fabulous, Marge. Are you sure you can spare it?'

The doctor chuckled as she placed the appetising snack before them. 'To be honest, we're sick to death of quiche. We've been living off it since Reece came home. There hasn't been time to cook so I've just made up quiches and thrown them in the freezer. When we arrive back at the house we're all so shattered that the thought of organising food is repellent.'

'It's gorgeous.' Holly sighed, finishing it to the final crumb. 'Though I know what you mean about cooking after work. Thankfully I've no one other than myself to think about when I arrive home.'

Marge gazed at her thoughtfully. 'Have you never wanted to settle down, Holly?'

In the two years Holly had worked for the Caines she had never spoken of Martin, her ex-fiancé. Her CV, quite naturally, had given the details of her career—staff nurse in a training hospital in the Lakes for two years and a year as a DN in general practice before she had moved to Cornwall.

But the details didn't contain her personal history—the loss of her father when she was twelve and the move to the Lakes from Yorkshire, her birthplace, and finally, her mother's remarriage to her stepfather, Brendan. She had refrained from mentioning Martin simply because she did not want to invoke old memories. Cornwall and the challenge it had offered had been her fresh start both in a personal and professional sense.

'I was engaged once, just before I moved to Cornwall,' Holly admitted, awaiting the painful dart of remembrance which always accompanied Martin's memory, 'but I called off our wedding at the last moment.'

Marge's eyebrows lifted. 'Oh, my dear, that was a very hard thing to do, I'm sure.'

Harder than she had ever expected, Holly recalled. She still had nightmares about returning the wedding gifts and the cancellation of the church and hotel and the embarrassment of having to write to the guests they had invited. And, of course, above all else, there had been the terrible shock. Holly cleared her throat and looked up. 'I broke it off with

Martin a month before our wedding. It's an experience I would never like to have to go through again.'

Marge shook her head slowly. 'Oh, Holly. How awful for you— and for your fiancé, of course.'

Holly nodded. 'Yes. Yes, it was.'

At that moment there was a noise from the hall, and both women swung around to discover the tall form of Reece, standing in the doorway. Holly realised she must have left the door ajar when she'd entered the room and hoping her confidence to Marge had not been overheard, she rose and smiled. She reached across to the coffee percolator. 'Coffee, anyone?' she asked, hoping to deflect the awkward silence which seemed to fill the room.

'Not for me, thank you, dear,' said Marge, rising too and walking to the worktop. 'I'm hyped already from my three cups this morning—but you go ahead.'

Reece also refused the coffee and strolled to the window to stare up at the sky, his hands thrust deeply into his pockets. Marge lifted the remains of the quiche with a spatula and laid it on a plate, but just as she did this Reece turned to frown at her.

'If you're doing that for me, no, thanks, Marge. I wouldn't mind if I didn't see another quiche for the next fifty years.'

Marge laughed aloud and glanced at Holly. 'I told you so,' she barked, and with great fervour began to recall some of the more humorous aspects of the weight-reduction clinics she had taken.

After sitting with a newspaper for a few moments, Reece slid his fingers through his hair and made an effort to listen to his sister's conversation. As if finally admitting his inability to relax, he sighed and rose. 'I've one or two things I'd like to catch up with in my office,' he told them and, giving them a brief but vague smile, departed.

Marge was the first to speak. 'Ants in his pants.' She

chuckled. 'Was always the restless one, even as a boy. Still, he's a lot on his mind at the moment.' She sighed, suddenly hesitant, and, glancing at the closed door, added slowly, 'However, now we're on the subject, perhaps I ought to mention—'

Irritatingly, the door swung open yet again and, half expecting to encounter Reece again, Holly was relieved to see Tim bearing down on them, rubbing his hands appreciatively at the sight of food.

'I can see I've arrived at the right time,' he said, smacking his lips. 'Is that a leftover by any chance?'

Marge immediately forgot what she was about to say and leapt to deliver the last fragment of quiche. As the three of them sat and talked, Holly's mind lingered on Marge's last remark. Had she been about to disclose something about Reece? What it was she couldn't guess, but her admission about Martin and Reece's subsequent manner had triggered something in Marge's mind.

She supposed she would never know what it was now.

When Holly arrived downstairs at two o'clock Reece was in the waiting room, his head bent over a young woman who had slumped in her chair.

'I...I took a pill—penicillin, I think,' she mumbled, catching her breath. 'And afterwards I felt so funny I came back here.'

'Let's get you into my room.' Reece glanced up at Holly. 'She's inhaling air but exhalation is restricted,' he told her in a calm, professional tone, which made her wonder if she'd imagined the whole episode upstairs. 'Looks like a drug-related reaction.'

'It's Miss Gilbert, isn't it? Flora Gilbert?' The girl nodded as Bronwyn hurried across to see what was happening.

'Are you allergic to penicillin?' Reece asked, as they supported her towards his consulting room.

'I d-don't really know,' the girl stammered. 'I saw Dr Franklin this morning and he asked me the same question.'

'Is Tim still around?' Reece queried.

'I think he left about five minutes ago.' The last Holly had seen of him was when he'd shot off to do his house calls, after devouring the quiche.

Holly began to loosen the girl's clothing as she lay on the examination bench. Reece filled a syringe with adrenaline solution, after studying the notes which Holly had handed him. Ten minutes later, having administered the intramuscular injection, the crisis was over and the girl had recovered enough to sit up and drink a cup of tea.

'I have a chest infection,' Flora Gilbert explained, 'and the doctor asked me if I was allergic to penicillin. I didn't think I was so I said no. I suppose I must be. It all happened so quickly.'

'Well, you must remember from now on,' Reece told her firmly. 'It's essential you tell any doctor treating you. We'll put it down on your records but, nevertheless, it's a fact you must always state.'

'I never come to the doctors as I usually use homeopathic remedies,' admitted Flora.

Reece computed a fresh prescription. 'Oh, we do have our uses when all else fails,' he teased lightly, and Holly saw that the smile he gave the young woman had a visible effect on her recovery.

As he escorted his young patient to the door he stretched out a restraining hand to Holly as she also began to leave. As he touched her she flinched. For a moment their eyes met and tangled as a ripple of awareness slithered along her arm and made her jump.

'I promise this won't take very long,' he said quietly. 'Sit down, will you?'

For one moment she wondered if he was going to refer to what had happened in the staffroom, and in her confusion she knocked against the corner of the desk, only to be prevented from falling by his swift reaction as he reached out to save her. Supported in his arms, Holly stared at him. He seemed to be in no hurry to let her go.

CHAPTER THREE

'I'M SORRY, I tripped, I think,' Holly apologised—unnecessarily, for both of them knew she hadn't *chosen* to fall into Reece's arms. She was saved further embarrassment by Bronwyn's sharp knock and her reminder from outside the half open door of Reece's first patient.

Instead of releasing Holly, he kept his hand on her waist, his eyes intent on her face, and it wasn't until Bronwyn repeated her knock that he let her go and walked to the door.

Holly smoothed down her uniform, and while he was talking she stole a glance at him, trying to detect something in his voice or profile which might enlighten her as to what had just passed between them. When he turned around again, after addressing Bronwyn, his expression gave nothing away.

'I wanted to ask you about Peter,' he said. 'I would like to know whether, since the stroke, he has discussed the surgery with you, talked over any worries or concerns.'

Momentarily taken aback by this question, she frowned. 'Your brother doesn't confide in me, and if he were to,' she added carefully, 'I certainly wouldn't betray a confidence. Frankly, the best person to ask is Peter himself, isn't it?'

'You misunderstand me,' he said at once. 'I simply thought you might be able to shed light on matters which may be obvious to others and not so obvious to me. Here the positions are reversed—my viewpoint is subjective.'

She looked up him. 'As you think mine was with Jonathan?'

'I think we all have our Achilles' heel,' he replied with a faint smile. 'I was hoping you might be able to help me with mine.'

'I'm sorry...' she shrugged '...but I don't think I can.'

He studied her, as if deciding whether or not to believe her. For a moment she hesitated. She didn't care for this cat and mouse game. Why should he think she was privy to Peter's thoughts? And why was he asking in such a roundabout way?

She was about to attempt to clear the air when something made her decide to remain silent. Going on instinct, she decided to let the subject drop if he said no more. The silence was shattered by the ringing of the phone on his desk, which he moved to answer.

Lifting his eyes to the ceiling and covering the receiver with his hand, he sat in his chair to continue listening and mouthed, 'Patient with flu.'

Taking this as an opportunity to leave, Holly moved to the door. She glanced back as she opened it and was startled to meet his gaze as he seemed to be taking in her appearance. Her long-legged frame was encompassed in her dark blue uniform and neat belt, her shoulder-length hair was pinned back today with a black velvet Alice band and her eyes, as she met his, were wide, dark-lashed grey eyes which complemented her oval face and reflected an answering warmth in his own.

'See you later?' he mouthed again and, almost without realising it, she smiled and nodded. She received a similar response from him before he returned his attention to the phone.

Once back at Alison's small desk, she sat down and tried to understand the implications of what had just happened. She simply did not know what to make of her own reactions, let alone those of Reece. His behaviour in the staffroom had been distant and yet when he had saved her from falling she was certain she had detected…what? Had it been warmth and tenderness in his expression?

There was not, she decided, time for yet another bout of self-analysis. Since Reece had made an appearance in her life, she'd questioned herself enough about her motives. One thing was for sure—she had work to get on with and no amount of personal introspection would help solve her patients' problems.

When Holly arrived on Monday morning, a surgery for post-weekend traumas was in full flow. Not that Sunday hadn't brought a mini-trauma of her own in the form of a phone call from David who had sprained an ankle on Saturday when he'd tripped in the department store of which he was an executive manager.

She had listened to his woes for twenty minutes and had been shocked at herself for glancing at her watch, wondering if she would miss much of the afternoon film on TV.

As she pulled up and parked on the hill outside the practice, Holly still felt guilty at the wave of relief she'd experienced when David had postponed his next visit. However, this was soon forgotten as the new receptionist, Jo Stallbridge— a born chatterbox—happily supplied a potted history of her marriage, twin sons of eight and fisherman husband, Pat.

'Oh, by the way, Dr Caine said he'd accompany you tomorrow when things are quieter,' Jo finally remembered to tell her.

'Accompany me where?' Holly frowned.

Jo shrugged. 'Aren't you doing house calls together? It's in the book, anyway.'

Holly turned the pages of the visit-book and, sure enough, in red ballpoint Reece had marked his initial beside hers on follow-up visits to Mr Bevan and Ben Sharman.

For some reason she had put the thought of house calls

to the back of her mind, but now she saw Reece was intent on keeping to plan. And, indeed, the very next morning, Tuesday, he was there to meet her outside the practice. The soft breeze had turned into a fierce wind and she held onto her coat as her thick chestnut hair blew away from her face, leaving her grey eyes to water in the wind's cutting wake.

'Force eight on the coast,' shouted Reece, hunching his broad shoulders under his wax jacket. 'The local radio has just issued storm warnings—I think we may be in for some rough weather.'

'You may be needed here,' Holly ventured. 'Perhaps we should postpone visits for now?'

He shook his head, holding up the mobile. 'The girls will ring us if there's a panic.' He tilted his head towards the two cars parked on the slope of the hill. 'We'll take the Volvo again, if you don't mind—it's more of a workhorse in this weather.'

As the first clap of thunder groaned across the roofs of Cancreel, Holly found herself transferring her bags from the Fiesta and, with the packages safely stowed, she climbed in beside Reece.

The Volvo was just under a year old. Purchased before Peter had his stroke, Peter subsequently invested in an Audi, adapted to his disability. Now Reece drove the car expertly along the windswept lanes, the task made even more tricky by the torrential rain.

The green corrugated porch of Ben's cottage soon came into view and Ben opened the door as they knocked. 'Leave your coats on the banisters to dry off,' he told them. 'I've a fire going in the front room.'

It was an austere little room, an elderly settee and Ben's armchair comprising the only real furniture. There was, however, a pre-war crystal set which Ben had converted into a lamp and clean-as-a-pin brown linoleum over the floorboards. Above the hearth was a solitary map of the South China Sea, held in place by a knotted cord.

'They wanted to give me a colon-something.' Ben repeated the details of his brief stay in hospital. 'I said, no, thanks very much. Just put me back together as you found me and I won't bother you again. No colon-whatsits for me at my time of life.'

Reece bent forward, picking up the small shovel, to lift a toppled coal back into the fire. 'As I explained last week, Ben, a colonoscopy is just part of an investigatory procedure with a small fibre-optic camera. If you're not so keen, perhaps we can get to grips with handling a few of the other more local nuisances. How is the catheter?'

The old man snorted. 'To tell the truth, I'm fed up with the damn thing. I can't do without it and yet it's a blessed nuisance. Will you have another look at it for me?' He glanced at Holly. 'You don't mind, lass, if the doctor sees to it? This old man still has a smattering of his pride left.'

Reece glanced at her and she saw the amused gleam had come back into his blue eyes. Trying not to feel redundant, she found her way to the kitchen and filled the gas kettle, lifting the lid from the teapot in preparation for hot water.

Returning to the fire, she sat on the armchair with a sigh. Well, just because Reece seemed to have taken over her job, it didn't mean to say she couldn't revise some of the notes she had made on Ben. Taking out her folder, she reread her comments. Symptoms were difficulty in passing faeces, combined with diarrhoea, indigestion, tenderness in the lower part of the abdomen and loss of appetite. She noted there were several minor tests which Ben had refused, before discharging himself from hospital—after falling out with almost everyone!

Although Holly smiled at his fighting spirit, his refusal

of a colonoscopy was worrying. Ben's attitude was not just philosophical—it was fatalistic.

'Have we a smaller size than sixteen?' she heard Reece shout from the bedroom. Searching through her bags, she came up with a selection of catheters in their sterile wrappings which she had thought to bring along.

'Would you like any help?' she asked as Reece appeared around the door, his sleeves rolled up over brown forearms.

'Er…no, we seem to be coping, thanks.' He looked past her to the kitchen and, as if making an effort to cushion Ben's bluntness, said, 'But tea sounds good. Would there be a cup going?'

Raising her eyebrows, she smiled. 'I might just be able to manage that, I suppose.'

Retreating with a grin, he returned to the bedroom. Holly busied herself in the kitchen, waiting to pour their drinks until she heard both men emerge.

While sipping hot mugs of tea, the three of them sat in the flickering firelight. Ben settled himself in his chair and they listened to the retired mariner's fascinating sea stories. As Holly had heard before, life on the ocean wave had begun at fourteen when he'd bolted from home and joined a merchant ship. Soon bored, he'd dived for pearls with native divers and for his efforts had lost a pound of flesh to the jaws of a Great White. Older, thinner and wiser, he'd begun salvage work in the South China Sea. Remaining single, the pleasure boats of the West Country had occupied his last days of service. At sixty-five he had reluctantly bidden the sea farewell.

The subject of Ben came up later as, full of tea, they drove through more rain towards the Bevan house. 'Ben is young by today's standards.' Holly sighed. 'There must be a way to change his mind about hospital.'

'I don't think so,' Reece said leadenly. 'I found a lump, you see, lower right-hand quarter of the abdomen. It was painful, though he stubbornly maintained it wasn't. I opened my mouth to say I wanted him in but he shook his head before I uttered a word. He's made up his mind he's not going back in—whatever it is.'

'But all the more reason for those tests,' Holly protested, appalled at the thought of ignoring this new development.

Reece drew the car to a halt. 'Holly, I've done my damnedest. Other than carry him in physically, I just can't get him to listen to reason.' A sudden clap of thunder overhead caused him to look through the windscreen into the worsening weather. 'Anyway, it's no use going over it now. Let's tackle Eric Bevan—the wound was healing pretty well on Friday. Maybe we'll have better luck here.'

She could sense his intense frustration and she, too, felt thwarted. It seemed that even with all Reece's powers of persuasion Ben was intent on acting like an ostrich. However, she was not convinced. A female perspective, though not welcome in the case of catheters, might in this instance cause Ben to think again. She would give it a shot and call without Reece at some point in the near future— she certainly wasn't about to give up.

Holly redressed Eric Bevan's inguinal hernia repair and Reece, in a better mood now, pronounced it to be healing well. With repeated reminders to avoid lifting during the healing stage, they departed, the subject of Ben mutually adjourned.

Attempting to take the route back to Cancreel, Reece had to slow to divert from the flood which had cut off the road and they followed the signpost to Durnweston. The road thinned and as the wind shook the car Reece leaned forward, narrowing his eyes.

'What now?' he groaned, peering ahead. 'Looks like a tree down ahead.' He stopped the car and opened his door.

'Better take a look before we turn back. Perhaps there's room to squeeze by.'

No sooner had he left the car and walked the few yards to the felled tree than he was beckoning to her. Holly unlatched her seat belt and pulled on her mac, realising he was pointing to an object which lay amongst the leaves.

Careless of the driving rain, she ran to join him, and arrived to discover the prostrate body of a man but because of the density of leaves it was not clear whether he was trapped by the tree.

'Go back to the car,' Reece told her as he stripped off his jacket, 'and call the emergency services. Tell them they'll need some specialised equipment to lift this monster and to make sure they avoid the lower Cancreel road, which is flooded. Meanwhile, I'll get in there and see what I can do.'

Wasting no time, Holly ran back to the Volvo and made the call. She repeated Reece's warning to the operator, suggesting that tree surgeons and lifting equipment might be needed to deal with the tree. Then, taking Reece's case from the rear seat, she ran back through a fresh onslaught of rain.

'He's conscious, despite a head wound and possible sternal or anterior rib fractures,' Reece called to her as he pushed away the dripping leaves. 'It's not the trunk that's pinning him down, thank God, but a broken secondary bough. There's a chance we may be able to move it between us, but on no account take any weight. Just act as a guide as I lift.'

Holly nodded, following him back into the branches and wriggling herself into position against the wood.

'Don't strain, just push,' he warned. Pausing, he unexpectedly moved towards her to wipe the soaked hair from her face and with gentle fingers cupped her chin. 'And when this is over remind me to tell you just how lovely you look when you're totally drenched.'

Then he moved away and braced his chest against the bough, wrapping his own rain soaked arms around its girth. On the count of three, Holly pushed for all she was worth, the pounding of her heart coinciding with the rumble of thunder overhead.

'It's moving—leave it to me now,' Reece shouted. Lifting her head, she saw the ripple of tensed shoulder muscles rise under the transparent white cotton shirt. She had a brief, shocking glimpse of man exerting every ounce of strength against nature, his long, hard-packed and muscular body heaving and his arms and legs driving against the stubborn wood, which at last creaked ominously as it finally gave way to the determined human challenge.

'Don't move,' Reece panted as, bough dispensed with, he knelt down beside the accident victim and began to follow the vital pattern of emergency inspection—airway, breathing and circulation.

'M-my name's Neil Haigh,' the man wheezed later as Holly peeled off her mac and laid it under his head. 'I'm a f-farmer and was checking my herd when…' He held his chest and winced.

Reece gently fitted a neck collar, easing his patient with gentle movements. 'Don't worry, I can't find any spinal damage but I'm putting this on to be on the safe side, even though you seem to have full movement of your legs and arms.' Just then a siren wailed and Reece glanced at Holly. 'And not a moment too soon,' he muttered, reaching out to give her arm a squeeze.

The first paramedic clambered from the vehicle and Reece rattled off his findings as the farmer was transferred to the stretcher. 'Paradoxical respiration, possible pneumothorax and contusion to the head. He needs stabilisation of chest, high flow oxygen and fluid replacement.' Pushing his wet hair away from his face with his fingers, he frowned at Holly and his gaze ran over her in concern. 'You must be frozen, but would you mind if I asked you one last favour? Would you bring the Volvo if I go with them? Do you feel up to it?'

She was unable to stop herself shivering and her teeth were chattering, but she nodded and he slid an arm around her shoulders. 'Look, there's a towel and a jogging suit in the boot of the car. Make sure you dry yourself thoroughly and change before you attempt to drive. OK?'

She nodded again, touched by his concern. 'I'll be fine,' she reassured him. 'See you at Durnweston.' She smiled and accepted the keys as he pushed them into her palm, his fingers lingering over hers as he closed them.

After the ambulance had left she collected her mac and Reece's jacket from one of the police cars which had just arrived. Back in the Volvo she switched on the engine and heater full blast and rubbed the circulation back into her skin as she absorbed the warmth. It would do her no harm, she decided, to change when she arrived at the hospital where possibly she could beg a hot shower in the staff cloakrooms.

The Volvo was an easy vehicle to drive and, though tempted to hurry, she kept her speed low in the driving rain. Twenty minutes later, having parked the car by the ambulance bay, she saw the paramedic who had attended them.

'They're still in A and E,' he told her as he closed the ambulance doors. 'And it was lucky the doctor came with us—we had complications on the way back.'

'Is the farmer all right?' Holly queried.

The paramedic shrugged. 'It was fifty-fifty, I'd say. Why don't you go along? You look as though you could do with a hot cup of tea yourself.'

Holly thanked him and entered the hospital. She made

her way to the small ward office, where a kindly A and E nurse brought her a cup of tea. 'Do you know how Mr Haigh is?' Holly asked worriedly.

'Dr Caine intubated because of an undetected pneumothorax,' the nurse explained. 'He had to make a surgical incision in order to try to free the trapped air in the pleural cavity of the lung.'

Holly sighed and, resting in the chair, watched the nurse hurry away. She was grateful for the hot cup of tea, which revived her, and she applied herself to the wait, allowing her thoughts to linger sympathetically with Neil Haigh.

It was some while before she looked up to see the tall figure of Reece walk in. Wearily he sank into the chair beside her. 'He's going to pull through,' he said quietly and she gave release to a long sigh of relief. 'A branch must have breached the lung, although nothing was visible to us at the time. And if you hadn't helped me lift that bough from his chest he wouldn't be here to tell the tale.'

He reached across and took hold of her hands, encompassing them in his own. He looked at her, a frown slowly spreading across his brow. 'Now, will you please explain why you haven't changed out of those clothes, as I told you to?'

She was so relieved that his rebuke made her laugh. 'Oh, your stuff's not my style, I'm afraid. Far too flashy.'

'You've got a nerve. That's a brand new jogging suit. I'll bet you don't even know what colour it is.'

'Navy blue,' she said, 'and I never wear navy blue.'

He laughed, leaning forward to brush tendrils of hair from her cheek. 'Navy blue would suit you very well, but with your colouring I'm sure there are few shades you couldn't wear. Grey eyes and that gorgeous chestnut hair... It's a combination guaranteed to turn any man's head—even in the pouring rain.'

* * *

In the car park he cupped her elbow and steered her to the Volvo, ushering her into the passenger seat and closing her door. Seconds later he sat beside her and dropped something on her lap. 'Now, put this on until we get back. It's only the top half so we've compromised.'

She laughed softly but did as he said, opening the drawstring neck of the jogging top and pulling it over her head. She smoothed her hair on her shoulders as best she could.

'You see,' he growled, his eyes running over her with warm regard. 'I told you. Blue isn't flashy at all.'

She smiled as she looped the toggles. 'Navy blue reminds me of school, that's all.'

'And what's wrong with that?' he asked as he started the car. 'You looked like a schoolgirl this afternoon—damp hair, no make-up and a smattering of freckles. For a little thing like you to push the way you did—'

'Not so little,' she said, hugging herself as the heater once again warmed the car. 'Five-eight's quite tall and I'm not exactly waif-like.'

He glanced at her with an appreciative smile. 'Woman-like, then,' he murmured, making the colour flood to her cheeks. 'Very, very woman-like.'

To counteract her embarrassment she looked up at the sky and said the first thing that came to mind. 'I've forgotten what the sun looks like, haven't you?'

She felt his eyes on her. She dared not look at him, dared not meet those blue eyes, not the way she felt right at this moment, and when at last he turned his attention back to the road she gave a silent, aching sigh.

'There have been times this year when I've cursed the sun,' he said quietly.

She took a breath. 'Really? Why?'

'Oh, dust, dirt. Helicopters kick up so much surface soil you tend to get grit even between your teeth.'

She remembered what lovely teeth they were. White and even and strong, like his character.

'But, then, on the other hand, when you haul someone up from water that's below freezing you tend to revise your thinking,' he went on, almost as if speaking to himself.

'It sounds terrifying.' She shuddered, remembering how cold she'd felt during today's storm—mild in comparison with what he must have experienced.

He shrugged. 'Not terrifying, but sometimes...' He stopped, his voice tailing off as his face darkened.

'Yes?' she prompted, daring to turn and study his profile.

'Sometimes you wish there was more.' he murmured, his gaze locked on the road ahead but seeming to be very far-away, too. 'You do the best you can but then you have to switch off. You have to separate yourself from the situation and leave it to others to finish off. And it's worst with kids. You always wonder...'

'How they are?' she guessed.

He nodded. 'Often we deal with whole families—car smashes, planes, trains, boats. Families on holiday, travelling, playing, enjoying themselves one minute...and the next...'

Holly shuddered again. 'I don't know how you do it.'

'Oh, it's not all doom and gloom,' he said, quick to lighten his voice, and turned to smile at her. 'There are some very rewarding moments, too. When the rescue goes well it's a real success story, a great feeling.'

There was a depth to his voice which she had missed before, something that caused her heart to race at its intensity. She remembered Joshua and Josie and how instant the rapport had been, and she knew his experience of life had given him a communication ability that many people did not have with youngsters.

She sighed softly, bringing her gaze back slowly to the road. No wonder his attitudes in general practice were so

different. Now she understood him a little better. He
worked best under pressure—that was evident. She failed
to notice—because she was so distracted—that they had
taken the road not to Cancreel but eastward in the direction
of Chartwell House.

Holly frowned and sat up, surprised to see the elegant ga-
bles of the Caines' country home. With four generations of
Caines having occupied the house, Holly reflected that
Marge and Peter must rattle about in the place these days.
When they were younger, it had been a busy household,
according to Marge. The many stories she'd related of Drs
John and Catherine Caine's lively parties had created a col-
ourful impression in her mind.

John Caine, white-haired and still charming in his mid-
seventies, had passed away before she had arrived in
Cancreel. The funeral, she understood, had been the last
time Reece had come home. Catherine, their mother, had
died a decade before that, but Marge and Peter had always
talked fondly of old times. Why, then, wondered Holly as
she stared at the old house, had Reece so determinedly dis-
tanced himself from his roots?

'Chartwell?' she murmured, glancing at Reece. 'Are we
stopping to collect something?'

'No, but we had to come this way because of that flooded
road.' He shrugged lightly. 'Seemed sensible, as we were
passing, to stop for a shower.'

'But I've no fresh clothes, Reece,' she gasped. 'And I
can't wear your joggers. The bottoms will swamp me!'

He chuckled. 'Don't worry, you won't have to wear anything but your own clothes. Mrs O'Kief will have your
uniform washed and dried in no time. She's very sensibly
persuaded Marge to invest in one of these state-of-the-art
washing-machines.'

Holly had forgotten about the Caines' daily, whom she'd

met several times while visiting Peter during his convalescence. The mention of her presence in the big house was strangely reassuring, though she failed to see why. This wasn't a seduction scene—it was a very sensible suggestion on Reece's part.

He was already out of the Volvo, unlocking the heavy oak front door with its pretty panes of coloured leaded glass. 'Mrs O'Kief?' he called loudly as Holly followed him into the warm, wood-panelled hall.

The seemingly endless polished parquet and solid, family furniture could have been off-puttingly austere if the Caines hadn't made the place a home rather than a museum, treating it with the same casual affection as they did the surgery.

Her eyes lingered affectionately on the heaps of medical magazines, piles of old newspapers and thick scatter rugs. If it hadn't been for Mrs O'Kief, the housekeeper, Marge had often remarked, Chartwell House would have made a perfectly suitable recycling centre.

Reece frowned. 'She probably has the vacuum going somewhere in the house. While I find her, why don't you go ahead and use the guest room? It has an adjoining bathroom—there's a tub and a shower, whichever you prefer. Leave your uniform on the bed and Mrs O'Kief will see to it.'

'Are you sure?' Holly frowned at the long flight of stairs. 'I really don't want to put her to any trouble.'

He shook his head, grinning. 'Not at all. Your presence in the house will prove a welcome diversion, I suspect.'

Hoping this was so, Holly walked towards the stairs then stopped as she realised she had no idea where the guest room was.

'Is there something wrong?' Reece asked.

She laughed abruptly, looking back. 'Only that I don't know where I'm going!'

He frowned, almost as if he was surprised at this, but

then he lifted his arm and pointed. 'First right at the top, third door on the left. And shout if you can't find the soap!'

Holly glanced upwards, following his direction, but registered the remark and looked back sharply, only to find him gone. Of course he was joking—and why not?

She hesitated but began to ascend the stairs, almost expecting to see Mrs O'Kief's smiling face, but on reaching the top she was disappointed to find the long passageway deserted. Turning right, as Reece had instructed, and counting three doors to her left, she finally found the guest room which had lemony walls and pretty rattan furniture.

With one last, searching glance along the corridor, Holly abandoned hope of catching Mrs O'Kief. In the bathroom she undressed, placed her underclothes on the heated towel rail, draped herself in a towel and returned to the bedroom, placing both the jogging top and uniform on the bed.

She locked the bathroom door behind her and sighed with pleasure as she used a hand shower to wash her hair, borrowing a little shampoo from the dispenser. Then, running hot water into the deep, luxurious tub, she finally sank beneath the surface, leaned back on the comfortable headrest and dared to close her eyes.

The next thing she knew there was a loud, rattling noise. Someone's voice brought her shooting up from the water.

'Coming, Mrs O'Kief!' She clambered wetly from the bath and clutched the nearest towel, draping it around her sarong-style. Shooting the bolt she fully expected to see the small, neat figure of Mrs O'Kief waiting outside when she opened the door.

'Are you all right?' Reece demanded. 'I couldn't seem to make you hear me.'

She blinked. He stood there in a thigh-length green silk gown, his brown calves wet, feet in thongs and his hair pebbled with the remnants of shower water.

'I'm f-fine,' she stammered. 'Perfectly fine. I'm afraid I

must have dozed off in the bath.' His eyes shifted over her bath-pink skin, then lowered to the soft shadow of her breasts under the towel. Quickly she asked, 'Did you find Mrs O'Kief?'

'No,' he said quietly. 'I phoned the surgery to let them know where we were and Marge apparently gave her the afternoon off so I persuaded the washing machine into action before I showered. I've, er, left the finished article on the bed.'

Silence fell. Waves of heat emanated from his body as he reached up to touch her wet hair. 'All the threads are sparkling,' he whispered, 'like little trails of spun silk...gold and red and brown, each following its own path.'

Then slowly his hand moved up to gently lift her chin before he bent to kiss her, a kiss she had in some wonderfully mysterious way expected.

CHAPTER FOUR

FOR a moment the scent of Reece's freshly washed skin and touch of his lips stirred something buried deep inside Holly, something that had been missing for a long time in her life, and as he lifted his head she recognised the look in his eye, the look she had seen before. 'It wasn't my intention to kiss you…yet,' he murmured softly, 'but I'm afraid there's a certain temptation with you, standing there, in nothing but a towel.'

'Yet?' she echoed and felt a fluttering inside.

'Yes. I'd been thinking about it…' He leaned against the door, watching her. 'Today in the rain…but it didn't seem very appropriate in front of poor old Neil Haigh. But let's suppose I'd found the opportunity—would you have objected?'

She took a deep breath, then slowly let it go. 'I didn't mind just then…'

'And you wouldn't object to me kissing you once more?' He moved towards her but she held out her hands and as she felt her palms come into contact with his chest she shuddered.

'Reece, did you bring me back to Chartwell deliberately? Did you know Mrs O'Kief wasn't here?' Her heart was pounding so heavily she thought she might miss his answer but he stood still and, hesitating, refrained from touching her.

'The answer to that is yes and no. No, I didn't plan to bring you here until the flood gave me the idea and, yes, when I called out Mrs O'Kief's name I suspected the house was deserted.'

'So that little story—'

'Was to put your mind at rest.'

'But not yours?'

He shook his head. 'My mind hasn't been at rest from the first day I saw you.'

She took another breath. 'I don't quite know what to say.'

'Either say I can kiss you again or stop me right now, Holly.'

She allowed her eyes to meet his and almost gave way to the yearning inside, but shook her head. 'I don't think so, Reece.' She felt dizzy with longing and the bedroom was but a few steps away. She only had to say one word and he would take her in his arms. So why not? It was a question which seemed to be reflected in his own eyes. She felt as though she had known him for years, for a lifetime, perhaps all eternity, a feeling contrary to all logic but still as real so why not just say yes?

'Do you want me to go?'

'I'm not quite sure what I want,' she admitted, 'today.'

His smile made her heart leap. 'Does that mean there will be a tomorrow?'

'There's always tomorrow,' she murmured.

'In that case…' he lifted his index finger, put it slowly to his lips and then transferred it to hers '…I can wait,' he whispered.

Reece was standing in the drawing room dressed in a soft green sweater and darker chinos when Holly came downstairs. His arm rested on the Adam-style mantelpiece and, not hearing her, he slid a hand into his thick, dark hair and smoothed it pensively over his head to the base of his neck where he slowly kneaded the muscle.

'Reece?'

He immediately straightened at the sound of her voice,

turning to look at her. His gaze went over her slender figure and long legs, the freshly laundered uniform and the cloud of chestnut hair which she had towelled and brushed until it was as good as dry. Having no moisturiser with her, she'd used the dispenser of body cream and her face had a shiny, youthful look, her eyes a doubtful, vulnerable grey as she looked uncertainly at him.

He held out his hands. 'Come and warm yourself.'

She walked over and slipped her hands into his. The heat of the gas fire radiated through the natural-looking coals in the old hearth.

'Would you like something to eat?' he said quietly. 'There's enough time for a sandwich if you'd like one.'

She shook her head. 'No, thanks, I'll eat later at home.'

'You'll have to borrow a sweater of Marge's or something for the return journey. Both our coats are the worse for wear. I'll have them cleaned tomorrow.'

'Oh, yes, thanks. Perhaps I—' She stopped in mid-sentence, gazing up into his watchful face. What was she to say? What kind of chemistry was being generated between them? Assuming it wasn't just going to go away and they both felt the same, what were they to do about it?

'I think,' he said, 'the sooner you and I decide to talk about what's going on between us the better.'

She lifted her eyes slowly. 'Reece—'

He stiffened. 'You're going to tell me you're in love with Peter?'

She was so surprised by this she almost laughed. 'Whatever makes you think that?'

He shrugged. 'You seem very close.'

She hesitated. 'In a professional sense—I would hope so.'

'And in a personal one?' Before she could reply he had pulled himself up straight, his brow creased. 'I expect you are about to repeat that you're not aware of Peter's deeper feelings?'

'No,' she answered truthfully, 'I'm not.'

'And David?'

'David?' Again she almost laughed. 'You make it sound as though there are handfuls of men in my life, Reece. And even if there were, which there aren't, I don't think you have the right to question me.'

He looked down at the fire, his mouth tightening. 'No, you're quite right, I don't. But I wondered—'

'If all these mythical men in my life had anything to do with my refusal to be seduced today?' She couldn't hide the hurt in her voice and she tried to draw away her hands, but he gripped them tighter, bringing her gently toward him.

'I'm sorry,' he said softly. 'I didn't mean it to sound like that. I'm just—' He shrugged and shook his head slowly. 'Best we give up on today, don't you think? It has been pretty shattering.' He smiled. 'In more ways than one.'

She smiled, too, but inside she felt lost and out of her depth. Knowing the strain of the day was telling on them, she was relieved when he bent to sweep a warm looking cable-knit sweater from a chair.

'Here, take this for the time being.' He drew it warmly around her shoulders. 'It's Marge's. You can return it to her tomorrow in surgery.'

His fingers brushed softly against her hair and, all too aware of the current that ran fiercely between them, she pulled the sweater around her, before walking ahead.

In retrospect the stop-over at Chartwell House and what had happened there seemed so far removed from her ordinary life that the rude awakening of a packed teatime surgery seemed somehow reassuringly familiar. With Peter and Tim in surgery, Reece hurried to his room to conduct

an emergency hour while Marge left to make the outstanding house calls.

Checking the nurse's book and finding only one call,
which could be done in the morning, Holly decided to head
for home. Not seeing Reece again, she stopped for some
pasta and bread on the way and tried to put him out of
mind—for the evening at least— by phoning her mother in
Cumbria.

Sara Lewis occupied almost an hour of her daughter's
time with news of the hotel she ran with Holly's stepfather,
Brendan. Although David's name was mentioned, Holly
had no interest in discussing the Longshaws.

David was the son of Jocylyn Longshaw, her mother's
friend. It had been at Jocylyn's birthday celebration just
over a year ago that David had asked Holly to go sailing
with him. More to please her mother, she reflected, she had
accepted. Holly knew her mother's concern for her was
deepening for after the break-up with Martin and her subsequent move two years ago from the Lakes Holly had
thrown herself into work almost tirelessly. Sara Lewis, doing her best to matchmake, had asked Holly and David to
stay at the hotel at Christmas. Not only had the idea not
appealed, but bumping into Martin and his wife would have
been likely in the lakeside town in which they all still lived.

Too mentally exhausted after the phone call to do very
much more than to go to bed, Holly slept better than she
thought she would. At least her mother's machinations—
and avoiding them—had prevented her from thinking of
Reece!

By morning the gale had blown itself out. A blue sky and
pale November sun transformed Cancreel, though the
streets were strewn with debris and the villagers were out
early to inspect the storm damage.

As she parked the Fiesta and walked across the road to

the surgery, she wondered what damage, if any, had been done to her working relationship with Reece. Perhaps it was just as well their conversation had come to an end when it had yesterday. Part of her resented being questioned about Peter and David and she was disquieted by this, aware that her feelings for Reece had yesterday somehow moved away from the professional level to something far more intimate.

She walked less confidently into the practice, aware of the strange sensation of fluttering behind her ribs which always seemed to coincide with Reece's appearance. However, finding him not there, an equally perplexing mixture of relief and disappointment soon overshadowed this.

Jo was on duty at the desk, coping with the post-storm crisis. Making her way first to the staffroom, which was also deserted, Holly left the borrowed sweater on the worktop and enclosed a small note of thanks. On returning to Reception, she heard Jo's voice rise in panic.

'I'll ask Dr Caine for you if only you'll just sit down for a moment. He's with a patient at present.'

'And how long am I supposed to wait?' an irate woman demanded of the new receptionist. 'This is ridiculous. I've a family to see to and a husband to get off to work.'

'I'm sorry we're so busy,' Jo apologised, unaware that the signal from Peter was in operation.

'I think Dr Peter is ready for his next patient,' Holly pointed out as the green light flashed.

'Oh—gosh, yes. Mrs...?' Jo seemed to go blank. The computer screen gave several blips as her fingers careered over the keyboard.

'I'm next!' shouted a woman in a headscarf.

'No, it's me,' interrupted a man in a fisherman's jersey.

'Isn't Bronwyn with you this morning?' Holly asked.

Jo shook her head. 'The storm blew the roof off her garage. She's unearthing her car at the moment. I'm here by myself for a bit and, to tell the truth, my mind's just gone blank.'

'Perhaps I can help until she arrives,' Holly suggested, mentally shuffling the calls she had to make, aware that Jo couldn't be left alone safely.

'Oh, would you?' Jo rolled her eyes.

Holly smiled and walked to the far end of the desk to confront the lady in the headscarf who looked as if she were about to explode.

'My name's Hilda Mayer,' barked the woman. 'I was booked in for a cervical smear last week with the nurse and when I arrived, I was told she was off sick. Now I come again and she's still not here.'

'I'm afraid Alison will be late in this morning.' Jo caught Holly's attention, discreetly pointing to a note on the desk in Alison's handwriting.

Holly nodded, glancing back at Mrs Mayer. 'I'm Holly Edmunds, the district nurse, not the practice nurse, but if you've no objection I'll be happy to help.'

'Doesn't seem as there's much choice,' muttered the woman, and with a final snort strode away into Alison's room.

Jo giggled. 'Good luck. I think you'll need it.'

Holly made a face. 'I'll be through in ten minutes—hopefully. If I'm not out by then you've permission to come in and drag me out. By the way, where is Alison?'

'Delayed with the kids, I think,' whispered Jo with a gleam in her eye. 'Perhaps she knew she had to face Mrs Mayer this morning.'

In Alison's room Mrs Mayer was waiting, her gaze fastened on her watch. Holly went through the formalities of the brief health and blood-pressure check and then asked her patient to remove her lower clothes and lie on the examination bench. Obviously used to the routine Mrs Mayer was up on the bench in seconds—before Holly had even donned gloves. Taking the sterile speculum and carefully gathering a swab specimen, Holly completed the smear without complication.

'The results are usually though in three to four weeks,' she explained when Mrs Mayer had dressed.

'More like six, you mean. And then it takes you a good half-hour to find them. I've learnt my lesson. I never ring in. My phone bill would be astronomical. I come here and make sure they're looked for in the right place.' Without a backward glance or a word of thanks, the woman strode from the room.

Holly hoped this might be the last of the agitated patients but as she walked into Reception there were more raised voices.

'I've been waiting three quarters of an hour,' one patient was complaining.

Holly glanced at the computer screen. 'Marge is running late,' Jo observed worriedly.

'I'm sorry,' Holly apologised. 'The storm caused rather a lot of problems this morning.'

'I managed to get here on time—so should the doctor,' muttered the man as he returned to his seat.

Just then a young man with a blood soaked rag tied around his forehead swayed over the desk. 'Could someone see me? I'm feeling a bit sick. I think I n-need to lie down—'.

Holly shot around from behind the Reception counter as she saw the hazy pupils dilate. The fact that he was six feet of muscle hadn't occurred to her until he almost collapsed in her arms. If Reece hadn't been there to take his weight she realised that both of them would probably have gone crashing to the ground.

'It's all right, I've got him,' Reece said, pulling the big man's arm around his shoulders and leading him to his room. Lowering him into the chair, he urged him to open his knees and lower his head between them.

Reece glanced at Holly and smiled the kind of smile which made her heart turn over as he lifted a teasing eyebrow. 'You'll need some building up if you're intent on hauling six footers around the place.'

'Well, at least I would have cushioned his fall.' She laughed, relieved the tension between them had been broken.

Their patient also seemed to see the funny side of things. 'I'm laughing because otherwise I'd be crying,' he said, still with his head bent. 'You see, I can't stand the sight of blood. I'm a roofer—ask me to go up any height and it won't bother me, but blood gives me the creeps. Especially my own.'

'Then we'll try not to spill too much of it.' Reece grinned. 'But, by the looks of that gash, we're going to have to stitch.'

'Oh, no,' the roofer groaned. 'Not stitches.'

Reece's mirthful gaze caught Holly's before he patted the man on the shoulder. 'Don't worry, they'll only be small ones. You're registered here, I take it?'

Their patient nodded. 'Name's Mike Long. Haven't been for ages. Blood, needles—anything like that—I hate.'

'Yes, you did mention it.' Reece's eyes were still filled with amusement as he turned to Holly and asked her to find the patient's records. Unearthing them from the office, she brought them in and laid them on the desk just as Reece completed his examination under one of the lamps.

He frowned. 'How in the world did you do it? This cut is jagged as well as deep.'

'I thought it was safe to go up a two-floor building,' he responded, as Holly carefully cleaned the awkward wound, after washing her hands and slipping on gloves. 'I wanted to check the scaffolding before anyone else arrived. I needed to make sure none of the lads ran into trouble, but a gust of wind came up from nowhere and brought down a roof tile.'

'Well, you were lucky it didn't catch your eye.' Reece held out his hand for the lignocaine. 'What kind of structures do you work on?'

While occupying the man's attention, Reece infiltrated the anaesthetic. Mike Long was so taken up with his tale of a crumbling cathedral spire he barely noticed the needle's swift entry. After the area had become numb, Reece sutured the edges of the skin neatly together. 'All done. That wasn't so bad, was it?' he said with a grin.

'As a matter of fact, no,' said the big man. 'I expected it to be much more painful.'

'Brave man.' Reece chuckled. 'Now, don't forget to make an appointment with the receptionist to have those stitches out in a week's time.'

Holly turned her attention to clearing the trolley as the two men walked to the door. She hoped Mike Long would distract Reece long enough to fill the gap before the next patient came in to avoid the chance of an embarrassing silence or an awkward conversation.

But after Mike Long had said good-bye Reece closed the door. 'Thank you for your help this morning,' he said quietly. 'It was much appreciated. We seem to be spectacularly short of staff and with double our quota of patients.'

'I'm happy to be of some help,' she replied, adding quickly, 'Have you heard anything from Durnweston?'

He nodded. 'Neil Haigh's made a good recovery. I've a feeling the gods smiled on us yesterday.'

She looked into his eyes uncertain of his meaning, and in a flash of understanding saw he was not referring to Neil Haigh alone. There was no chance to say more as Jo, with another sharp knock, came bursting into the room, followed by the angry man who half an hour previously had complained he had been waiting for three quarters of an hour.

Leaving Reece and Marge to the busy surgery, Holly left for her calls as soon as Alison and Bronwyn arrived. She tried to focus on Jonathan, clearing all other thoughts from mind and attuning herself to the situation which would be presented to her when she arrived.

But the technique she had learned to master over the years somehow eluded her as her thoughts stubbornly drifted back to Reece and the smile which had put paid to any thoughts she'd had of treating him with professional coolness.

What might he have said to her this morning if Jo had not entered? Then she was annoyed with herself for speculating. What could be achieved through any amount of talking? The facts were that he was in England for six months, two of which had almost gone. He had a life of his own on another continent on the other side of the world—and it had nothing to do with her.

Besides, what was she thinking? After Martin, she'd decided that her career came first and she'd done everything in the last two years to carve out her independence. Real independence. With a home of her own and a job she loved, with security...real security.

Her frown deepened. She had, without knowing it, switched off the engine and was gazing sightlessly at the Avis bungalow. Gathering her bags, she locked the Fiesta and was met at the door by Gwen who immediately burst into tears at the sight of her.

'Jonathan's so depressed,' she sobbed. 'You see, Gary didn't turn up. His road manager phoned to say they're off on a world tour. He hasn't got time to see Jonathan or even speak on the telephone before he leaves. Oh, Holly, Jonathan lives for Gary's visits. Now it's plain Gary doesn't want to be bothered with him any more.'

Holly made her way to Jonathan's bedroom and found him staring into space. She drew up a chair and tried to gain his attention, but it was as if he didn't see or hear her, having withdrawn into his own silent world.

It was a problem which she knew she would have to make Reece aware of, she reflected as she drove to the Bevans', tormenting herself with the knowledge that Reece had foreseen the possibility of this happening and, had she not been so determined to plead the family's cause, she would have seen it too.

With no new developments arising with Eric Bevan, she made the call she had left from yesterday to an elderly lady in need of dietary advice. Once the call had been completed she turned the car to the cliff road and Ben Sharman. To her surprise, Ben said he felt much better. He made her tea and served a slice of cake made by his home-care worker. Holly wondered if his cheerfulness was genuine. He even allowed her to check his catheter and, while doing so, she asked the all important question regarding hospital.

'We'll see,' he said, and this she took as an indication he'd given positive thought to clinical investigations. At last she was making headway. Even the catheter didn't seem to be troubling him so much—perhaps she really had succeeded with Ben.

Feeling she could now return to surgery armed with a little good news to balance Jonathan's troubles, she drove back to the village less apprehensively. However, when she arrived only Marge was in her room, preparing to leave on her visits. With a quick exchange of news she discovered Peter had gone early, leaving Reece to do the outstanding house calls.

Feeling the need to expound the new developments with Jonathan, Holly explained the events of the day to Marge, who seemed sympathetic but soon left for her own calls.

Holly stared bleakly at the cleaner as she began her nightly toil and realised there was no where to go now but home.

It was clear there would be no peace for her tonight and she sighed, thinking of the long hours that stretched ahead. She realised how much she depended on Reece's comments, sometimes challenging, sometimes conflicting, but always decisive. No other member of staff created the kind of feedback Reece provided and now she missed it.

Eventually she wrote a brief note. Making no excuses, she clearly stated her failure to foresee the Gary Sharpe incident and the potential disaster she had not been able to avert. She left the note on his desk, where he was bound to see it at some point.

Holly's team leader had called a meeting for the end of the week. Because it was due to be held at the clinic in Durnweston, Holly phoned in to the surgery next morning to explain.

'Well, you've nothing urgent here,' Bronwyn told her. 'Dr Reece Caine is going to see Jonathan Avis—he's marked himself a visit. Apart from that, you're free. Did you want to go with him?'

Holly hesitated. 'Not unless he's requested it.'

'No. He didn't mention it to me.'

'In that case, I've a team meeting this morning, Bronwyn, and then I'm going to Dr Napier's surgery. Unless you want to ring me in the event of an emergency I'll see you Monday.'

Holly replaced the phone, ignoring the temptation to ring Gwen. Reece was making a visit so she had better leave it at that. He hadn't asked to see her, though he must have read her note. She must now leave it up to him, despite the almost overpowering sense of responsibility she felt.

At the team meeting Holly reviewed her caseload with Helen Joyce and her other colleagues, all of whom worked widespread areas. Dr Napier's surgery and the Caines were her priority, though seventy five per cent of her work revolved around Marge's and Peter's larger practice. The community nursing team were more involved with Dr Napier, an older man, due for retirement, with just one younger partner.

After discussing Jonathan in particular, it was decided that, in liaison with Reece, the health visitor should call, a female colleague who, Holly knew, was acquainted with Jonathan's case.

Holly left photostats of her report with Helen and made her final call on Dr Napier. She tried to put Jonathan to the back of her mind, telling herself she had done all she could. And possibly by now, to put her mind at rest, Reece would have left a message on her home answering machine.

Certain that was what had happened, she drove home swiftly. Her heart picked up speed as she saw, in the front room by the window, a green light, flashing on the machine. Pressing the recall button, she heard the computerised tone and then the sound of a male voice. With a sharp pang of disappointment she identified it as David.

She met David that night in the foyer of the Harbour Hotel. Dressed in a formal dark suit, he suggested cocktails, which she declined as she was driving. Therefore, avoiding these preliminaries, they were soon seated at their table.

Holly chose a consommé and Dover sole with marinated vegetables, but she could hardly contain her surprise when David ordered champagne. 'To us,' he toasted as he raised his glass. Then, drawing a small gift-wrapped box from his pocket, he slid it across the table.

Holly's heart sank. She opened the gift, slowly peeling off the dainty wrapping. Inside the box were three glimmering stones set on a golden band.

'An engagement ring?' she gasped.

'I've excellent career prospects,' David said as she tried to catch her breath. 'We can buy a property in the Lakes, and after we're married we can plan for a family as soon as you give up nursing.' He frowned, suddenly aware of her silence. Gently Holly closed the lid of the box. She looked up and wondered if she had ever considered that he might propose. They had, after all, been seeing each other for a year, and although she had never intended it she real-ised now he had obviously read more into their relationship than she. With a wave of guilty dismay she recalled Reece's remarks.

'Oh, David,' she sighed, looking up. 'The ring is beau-tiful—and I'm flattered you've driven all the way down here in the middle of the week just to propose to me but I'm afraid I just can't accept your ring.'

'But why not?' David's face was shocked. 'We've been seeing each other for long enough now. We've always en-joyed each other's company. Your mother said—'

'My mother means well, David, and so does yours, but you shouldn't be persuaded by them.'

'But I do want to marry you!'

She shook her head slowly. 'You want to *be* married and that's a different thing. You talk about a house and a life together as though it were one of your weekend exercises. But you can't plan a marriage by a map. It's unpredictable and uncharted. Love is like that.'

'Love?' said David woodenly.

'Yes.' Holly smiled softly, knowing the only person David would ever really care for was himself. 'You aren't in love with me and I'm not in love with you.'

He looked accusing. 'Is it Martin still?'

Her smile drained away. 'No, David it's not.' She real-ised, with more of a shock to herself than to David, that she hadn't thought of Martin for weeks, and certainly he had nothing to do with her decision now.

'I think,' she said quietly, looking at David's sullen features, 'it would be nice if we could part as friends.'

As the meal came to an abrupt and awkward end, Holly knew there was little chance of that after tonight. It was only much later, when she dragged herself in through the front door, that she allowed herself to give a deep sigh to relieve the tension she had imprisoned all evening.

David had been upset, though Holly felt it was more a case of his pride being hurt. With Martin she had shared a caring relationship, but with no grand passion. Looking back, she realised they had probably known each other too well for too long. Their expectations had been too ground based, too material, and, to a lesser extent, the same had happened with David. How could she possibly have allowed these misunderstandings to happen? Had she led David on? Had she ever given him reason to think she wanted marriage?

She sank wearily into a chair, bothering only to switch on the small table lamp. In the dim glow she leaned back. Had she done right in refusing David?

The answer made her shudder with sudden self-awareness. She had not known what it was to remember someone's touch, as she had Reece's, or to lose herself in a yearning which obliterated all other memories from mind. And, despite his avoidance of her recently, her thoughts were never far from the memory of the way she had felt in his arms.

CHAPTER FIVE

HOLLY spent Friday at Dr Napier's, filling in for a community nurse who had flu, and there was no word from Reece over the weekend.

On Monday and Tuesday she missed him altogether as he was out on visits each time she called at the surgery, but there were, however, visits marked out to Jonathan on the Saturday and Monday with Reece's initial against them, but with no word left from him in response to her note.

On Wednesday morning Bronwyn called her to the desk as she walked in. 'Thought you might like to know the rumour is we're to have another full-timer here on the desk and a new practice nurse is starting.'

Holly's grey eyes widened. 'But what about Alison?'

'Oh, she's still coming in, but her hours are being cut, I think. Marge told me yesterday.'

'But Alison's worked the same hours for years. Why would they want to cut them?'

'Well, I think—' Bronwyn started.

She stopped talking as a voice beside them said, 'Good morning, stranger.'

Holly's heart sank as she looked up into Reece's face, noticing first the cool tone of his voice. 'If you've a moment when you're ready?' he added, before turning and walking back to his room. The two women stared after him.

'What,' said Bronwyn with a frown, 'was that all about?'

'It's called facing the music,' Holly sighed. 'Except it won't be music—more like the gnashing of teeth.'

Bronwyn's face sobered. 'Oh, dear, really? It's been a horrid six months, hasn't it, since Dr Peter's stroke?'

Holly grimaced. 'Organised chaos, you mean?'

'Something like that,' Bronwyn agreed. As a voice issued impatiently from the waiting room, she called, 'Mrs Bailey—Dr Franklin's ready for you now.'

As Holly followed Reece to his consulting room she feared that the situation with Jonathan must have worsened, but why hadn't Reece been in contact with her? If she was honest, it wasn't only their patient she was worried about. Had Reece's silence meant he'd regretted what had happened at Chartwell?

At Reece's door she took a deep breath and walked in. He was busy with correspondence but looked up from his desk to gesture to the chair, making an abrupt movement with his hand.

Sensitive to this, she shook her head. 'No, I'd rather not.'

He frowned up at her, his eyes a flash of brilliant, ice-cool blue, and she hovered undecidedly until a smile edged its way across his lips. 'Perhaps you'd like me to ask Bronwyn to come in and chaperone us?'

Gazing into the vivid blue pools, which suddenly had a tiny spark of warmth in them, she sat. 'Oh, I think Bronwyn's got far too much to do at the moment.'

He lifted one black eyebrow. 'So...I'm to take it you've relinquished interest in the Avis family?' he said challengingly.

'I beg your pardon?'

'What else am I to conclude? I haven't seen anything of you over the last few days—in fact, all I had was this.' He waved her written note in the air.

'You weren't here when I came back from Jonathan's on Thursday,' she began to explain, 'so I wrote you the note. I also spoke to Marge—and then to Helen, my team leader—'

'But not to me,' he interrupted. 'Holly, I had the impression we were working with each other, not against. I

thought—and I'm sorry if I drew the wrong conclusions—
we'd finally come close to understanding one another.' He
sat back in his chair, narrowing his eyes. 'Was I wrong?'

Was he referring to what had happened at Chartwell? she
wondered. She felt the colour fill her cheeks as she shook
her head. 'No...no. I just assumed you would contact me
as soon as you had visited Jonathan.'

'Which I did on Friday, but I didn't see you all day.'

'Because I was at Dr Napier's. The community nurse was
off sick.'

'And Saturday and Sunday, too?'

She glanced up in surprise. 'But that was the weekend.'

'Did it make any difference? There was the phone. You
could have rung me at home.'

'Reece, I don't understand. I assumed you would contact
me— '

'I tried. I called after visiting Jonathan on Saturday morning. You weren't at home. Then I rang on Sunday and got
no answer. Not even the dratted answering machine.'

She opened her mouth to make some retort and then
closed it as she remembered that on Saturday morning she
had gone for groceries and on Sunday had left the answerphone off all day as she was at home. He must have rung
while she was in the garage, reorganising the chest freezer
as a result of her shopping trip the day before.

'Am I making any sense?' he said quietly. 'You can see
what's been going through my mind, can't you?'

The wave of relief that washed over her was so great
that she was just able to smile. 'Yes, yes, I think so. But,
you see, I thought you were avoiding me. I mean, after
what happened.'

He paused, before lifting his shoulders in a sigh. 'After
what happened we should have made time to talk. And we
didn't.'

She nodded. 'I'm sorry. But I really didn't know what to think. And I've been so worried about Jonathan.'

He stared at her, then smiled slowly. 'We'll come to Jonathan next but, first, when am I going to see you?'

Her heart missed a beat as he added quickly, 'Tonight and tomorrow I'm on call. But this is my weekend off. What if I pick you up on Saturday morning? We'll drive into the country and go somewhere for lunch.'

'Saturday...'

'You've nothing arranged?'

'No...no, but—'

'It's settled, then.'

Her eyes met his and she had no will-power to object because she saw he wasn't going to take no for an answer. And why should she say no? What was she fighting against? He hadn't propositioned her, for heaven's sake! All he'd suggested was that they talk—and eat lunch.

Before she could speak he had begun to talk again and it was a few seconds before she could drag her mind back to the conversation.

'Now, about Jonathan. Perhaps what happened with Gary Sharpe is really an opportunity for us. What if we could stimulate his interest in something else other than motor-bikes?'

For a moment she looked at him in confusion. 'Something else? But Jonathan's life has centred around motor-bikes for so long!'

'Well, that life is over now,' he said sharply. 'He has to come to terms with his limitations and begin again, albeit from square one. I see no reason why he couldn't, with something like a computer, begin to carve out a new inter-est for himself. After all, this is supposed to be the tech-nological age.'

'A computer?' Holly raised her eyebrows. 'Gwen and

Doug would never be able to afford such an expensive item.'

Reece shrugged. 'What do you think of the idea, leaving the finance to one side for the moment?'

It was an idea which Holly hadn't considered, but Brendan, her stepfather, had installed computers in the hotel and used the facility to link with other hoteliers abroad. It was certainly one way of communicating.

Holly nodded slowly. 'I see the sense in it, but where do we start?'

'Don't you collect his racing magazine every month? There are dozens of computer magazines on the shelves. What about taking one or two along at the same time?'

Holly paused. 'Do you think he would be interested?'

Reece shrugged. 'Who knows? It's worth a shot, I would have said. Anyway, give it some thought over the next few days, will you?' Then he smiled, the smile which made her heart skip a beat every time. 'And don't forget Saturday,' he said softly. 'Eleven sharp.'

Back in Reception Bronwyn frowned at her. 'Was it as bad as you thought?'

Holly stared into space. 'No, it wasn't.' She couldn't help smiling to herself, wondering what Bronwyn would say if she knew the truth and trying to suppress the curl of excitement inside her. She shrugged. 'To be honest, I got off rather lightly.'

Bronwyn quirked an eyebrow. 'Isn't life full of little surprises?'

Reece was the biggest surprise of all, Holly reflected as she went on her way. Though her failure to foresee and avert a patient disaster had given her many hours of concern, apparently Reece had looked on it in another way altogether. Coupled with his assumption that she had tried to avoid meeting him, she had completely misread the situation.

It had been a very long time since she had felt this way. The knowledge that he was as attracted to her as much as she was attracted to him increased both the apprehension and pleasure she felt at the prospect of Saturday. What could ever come of it? a small voice inside asked. It was a voice she chose to ignore, blanking off her mind as the excitement grew and grew.

Holly caught her breath as she drew the curtains of her bedroom window on Saturday morning. Nothing could have prepared her for the dramatic sight of snow falling in light feathery drifts, covering the roofs of the terraced houses opposite and filling up the windscreens of the vehicles parked in the narrow street.

At that moment the phone rang downstairs and she flew to answer it, her heart pounding as she wondered if it was Reece, phoning to cancel. It *was* Reece.

'Wrap up warmly,' he told her, making her spirits soar again. 'We're taking the toboggan.'

'But where?' She laughed. 'It's only a little bit of snow.'

'Pick you up in a couple of hours,' he said evasively, and left her wondering exactly what he'd meant by tobogganing. Rushing a breakfast of cereal and juice, she chose warm black ski-pants, black booties and a new roll-neck jumper in an oyster wool which she turned fashionably over the collar of her multicoloured ski-jacket. When Reece collected her at eleven she had just finished pinning her hair into a knot. He stared in open admiration at her tall, slender figure as she greeted him on the doorstep, a few misty flecks of snow driving in on her face.

His dark hair was scattered with tiny snowflakes and even his long black lashes had gathered snow. Like her, he wore a ski-jacket, though his was a deep sea green with a blue contrasting hood. He stamped his booted feet on the path to keep warm.

'You look wonderful,' he said, 'and the weather's wonderful. Come on, let's make the most of it. Are you ready?'

She reached for her bag, gave one last glance back into her cosy home and locked the front door. She ran with him to the Volvo and fell, laughing, into the passenger seat, having ducked a snowball.

'Won't the roads be treacherous?' she asked as he drove the Volvo carefully up the hill and out into the narrow lanes.

'Want to chicken out?' He grinned at her as the diesel engine pulled them onward, the coastline gradually receding behind them.

'We might get marooned,' she said with a laugh, her heart fluttering with excitement.

'We might,' he agreed, mischief in his eyes, 'but we've always got the toboggan.'

'Have we?' She glanced suspiciously in the back seat.

'It's in the boot. Did you think I was joking?'

'Now I know you're not,' she laughed. 'Where are we going?'

'A place called Penwarrell, near Padstow. Right on the river.'

'Padstow! Do you really think we'll get that far in this weather?'

'As long as we keep to the main Wadebridge road. And if we get stuck there overnight...' He left the sentence unfinished and shrugged, keeping a straight face. Then he took his eyes from the road for a second and gave way to laughter. 'Don't worry, I'm only teasing. I'll get us home safely.'

She sank back into her seat, laughing, too, although just for a minute the thought of becoming marooned with him at some little hotel in the country with six feet of snow between them and the outside world had a heart-fluttering appeal. But an hour later the Volvo had taken them safely down-country on the well-sanded road where traffic still kept up a steady pace, and it was not until Reece turned off at the sign marked Penwarrell that they found themselves once more in a winter wonderland.

The River Camel wound its way from the tiny Cornish port of Padstow, which in summer was popular with tourists for its golf and boating and the quiet charm that epitomised West Country life. Now the light dusting of snow transformed the picturesque estuary into a fantasy landscape, the craggy outcrops and tiny cottages like a scene from another planet.

'It's so beautiful and so strange,' Holly breathed as Reece turned the car into a lane which looked as though someone had laid a vast white sheet over it, with only the extremities of the hawthorn bushes pushing their spindly way through.

'Dad used to have a boat here,' Reece murmured. 'Moored it in the estuary—just a small cabin cruiser which we used for fishing. It was clinker-built and Peter and I would spend our summers doing it up and fishing. Dad would get down when he could find a locum and we'd stay at this place I'm taking you to. Marge and Mother would come sometimes, too—the people who owned it were friends. I remember they had a daughter, June. Peter, who was seventeen, was really keen on her. I remember wondering what could possibly entice him away from the boat. It's funny what comes back to you, isn't it?'

Holly nodded. 'Yes, yes, it is.' She hadn't expected this shared intimacy and somehow she felt moved that he should share it with her. She'd heard a lot about the Caines' parents from Marge, but now they seemed more real and she could imagine the family they had been, enjoying the summer holidays, spending time together away from the busy practice which John and Catherine ran together.

Reece let out a sigh at the next turning. 'Well, it *was*

here.' He engaged second gear and turned the wipers faster, peering through the windscreen. 'But it looks as though I've left it rather late to stroll down memory lane.'

Before them they saw the boarded-up shell of what had once been the small hotel that Reece remembered from his childhood. The five bar gate which blocked their way was chained and padlocked and the cluster of snow covered machinery in the drive appeared to be preparing for demolition.

'Which just goes to show,' Reece sighed, killing the engine, 'you can't turn back time.'

Impetuously, Holly reached out to clasp his hand, which had fallen to his thigh. 'Oh, Reece, I'm sorry. I know what it feels like. We did it once, Mum and I. It was in my second year of training and for some reason we went back to Yorkshire to see the house I was born in. But we couldn't even find the street. There was an industrial estate instead. It was as if those years with my father hadn't existed.'

He turned and lifted her hand and rubbed it between his own, then slowly he leaned across and kissed her softly, letting his lips linger until his forehead leaned against hers. Outside there was absolute silence. The snow fell in gentle, frothy flakes and began to build up on the glass.

'It looks as though we may need the toboggan after all,' he murmured, holding her grey eyes with his own brilliant blue gaze.

'You're beautiful,' he sighed huskily, 'too beautiful not to make the most of. Come on, let's go somewhere civilised and find ourselves a nice warm fire and a carvery.'

'I'm really rather warm already.' She smiled and raised her fingers to his face, smoothing them over his jaw, a jaw that fascinated her with its strength and sensuality, its perfect symmetry. He looked extraordinarily handsome, his dark skin tanned to a rich mahogany which highlighted the

vivid azure of his eyes against the white background of
snow.

'And so am I,' he muttered, and took her into his arms.
As her heart missed a beat he kissed her.

Holly always wondered how they had managed to reverse
from that sad little hotel and snow-filled lane and find their
way back to the main road. Somehow they did, although,
left to her, she would have gone on kissing him, loving the
tender feel of his lips and the exquisite flow of new life
which seemed to enter her body in that white paradise.

But Reece did the sensible thing and drove them back to
civilisation, where the snow had ceased falling and the
roads were wet, glimmering ribbons winding through valleys of white. They stopped to eat at a country hotel, sign-
posted from the motorway. They found a roaring log fire
and, as Reece had hoped, a small, traditional restaurant
where they ate roast turkey and apple pie and ice cream.

When the meal was over they removed themselves to the
deserted lounge and drank coffee from demitasse cups.
Little by little she told him about her childhood and the
death of her father when she was twelve from a coronary.
Of how her feeling of helplessness when he had collapsed
at home had sparked her desire for nursing and how the
tiny flame had been fanned by the need to make a life for
herself as she grew older and her mother remarried.

'And have you succeeded?' Reece asked her, lazily sipping his coffee, one knee hitched up and tucked behind the
other as he leaned back on the old cushioned sofa beside
her.

'Succeeded?' Holly frowned.

'To make a perfect life for yourself? Is there...anything
missing?'

She couldn't be sure if he was teasing her, but he was
far too perceptive for her to deceive. 'Well, I think I've

everything I aimed for—nursing, being part of a community—'

'But not sharing your life,' he persisted softly. 'Sharing it with someone?'

She looked down at her coffee-cup. 'In Cumbria, before I moved here, I was engaged,' she said quietly, 'but...it didn't work out...and since then...' She looked up into his face but he showed neither surprise nor curiosity. Instead, he lowered his own cup to the coffee-table and, taking the spoon, turned it slowly around in the rich brown liquid.

'And what about you?' Her question came softly, and she held her breath as she watched his face.

'There was someone once,' he said, shrugging, 'a long time ago.' He lifted his head and when he looked at her the pain she saw in his eyes made her realise he, too, had suffered. It was a pain which could not be disguised by words. 'It was before I left for America when I lived in London.'

'Not so long,' she murmured softly, 'that it still doesn't hurt to talk about it.' Her instinctive remark came out as more of a statement than a question. In response he finally slipped the spoon to the saucer and, reaching across to hold her hand, he grinned. 'Let's talk about something else, shall we—tobogganing, for instance? Or, better still, let's find ourselves a nice steep slope and plenty of snow.'

And they did just that. They drove to a local beauty spot, unearthed the toboggan from the boot and spent the last few hours of daylight hurtling down a hillside with dozens of other pre-Christmas revellers. Finally, satiated with snow and laughter, they drove slowly back to Cancreel, their headlights illuminating the flurries of snow which had begun to fall again. The powerful headlights pierced the darkness with a spectral eeriness as traffic slowed and thinned. Eventually luminous notices began to appear, indicating roads closed, diversions and warning signs.

'Still time for a marooning.' Reece lifted an eyebrow as they took the coast road to Cancreel. 'What are the odds on us making it home?'

She shrugged, her cheeks burning with colour from the fresh winter air, her hair, having long ago come loose in a snowball chase, cascading around her shoulders. 'Not good, I hope,' she sighed, 'because it will mean the day is finally over.' She wasn't afraid to admit it. Neither was she afraid to admit how content she was in his company or how much she enjoyed the cool blues music that drifted from the CD and their conversations on their jobs and families, all of which they had shared so naturally throughout the day.

'It doesn't need to be over,' he said, his voice low as he studied the road ahead. She gazed at his profile in the darkened car, his face lit by the instruments on the dashboard, and was astonished by the intensity of her need not to say goodnight but to go on discovering more about this man beside her, knowing as she had known from the first moment he had entered her life that he was in every way extraordinary.

Far too swiftly the Volvo crept its way into the snow-covered streets of the village and Cancreel, bolstered against the winter's snow, shed its evening rays languorously across their path until finally her small terraced house came into sight and her Fiesta, a great snowman on wheels standing by the kerb, winked welcoming lights in the Volvo's powerful beams.

'Do Volvos tend to freeze up easily?' she asked, and Reece looked at her with a frown at her question and then, seeing the smile edge slowly over her lips, his brow cleared.

'I think I'm about to find out,' he replied, and brought the car to a shuddering halt.

Holly wound her arms around Reece, welcoming him silently to her small, tidy bedroom with its pine furniture and white linen covers and treasures she had collected over the years. As she reached up to touch his face he caught her hand, brushing his lips over her fingers to precipitate the tell-tale stirrings of such desire that she was almost afraid to move.

He undressed her slowly, as though unwrapping an early Christmas present, sliding her sweater over her head and gazing at the soft swell of her breasts against the cream silk teddy. He lowered his head, kissed the smooth skin of her shoulders and slipped each strap with gentle fingers to free her from the imprisonment of her bra, sliding the flimsy underwear to the floor.

She was never quite sure afterwards if she undressed him or whether, in growing need of one another, the last remnants of their clothes were discarded in an anticipation which could no longer be restrained as the cool linen of the bed enveloped them.

'Holly, I have to ask...what we're about to do...runs a certain risk...' he said, holding still for one moment. As he hesitated she shook her head, wondering why she had not consciously thought of it herself.

'You're right,' she sighed, closing her eyes. 'And, of course, I'm not on the Pill.'

He pulled her gently towards him. 'At the risk of admitting I anticipated the situation...' he frowned '...while we were at the hotel today...'

She watched him leave the bed, watched his strong, lean body bend and retrieve his trousers, and her body shuddered with anticipation. When he moved back in beside her she was thankful that at least one of them had anticipated this moment, for postponing it would have seemed unbelievably cruel.

Their love-making was, as she had known it would be, beyond all her dreams as they entwined and coupled, hands and lips exploring curves of bodies, uninhibited by clothes and, once set free, transformed by desire that brought a cry of yearning from her throat.

He was tender and thoughtful, passionate and provocative, giving her pleasure before himself and for one fleeting moment she could not believe that her relationship with Martin had ever been possible. From the second Reece had begun to make love to her all memories ceased and her life began from the moment it should have sprung from—from him.

One hour slipped into the next. Her body awoke to his, lit first by an awesome fire they could no longer contain, and then in the early hours of Sunday the fire mellowed into embers as they lay, contented, in each other's arms, her head nestled into his chest, a chest covered in the darkest of hair and carrying his own male scent which rose softly into her nostrils.

Holly had wondered idly during the previous day if the ebony hairs which she had seen protruding from the green silk robe at Chartwell had travelled beyond the V which had been apparent to her astonished gaze, and she had been shocked at herself for wondering—but now she knew. She had lain against them and felt them prickle against her skin and drawn her fingers over the raised arrowhead that speared down his flat abdomen. Now she knew. Now she knew every inch of his long, muscular body, had entwined herself in its strength and mobility and had been brought to aching release as he had finally made her his own.

In the silent moments of the morning she fought back the little voice which made itself known, the voice which whispered, What happens now? How long do you have? In the dim light, warmed by his body and yet chilled by this voice, she shuddered. He moved beside her and wrapped his hands around her waist and, as if reading her thoughts, turned her towards him. 'No regrets,' he whispered. 'You mustn't lie there, having regrets.'

She looked into the blue eyes. 'No, no regrets, just thinking…'

He kissed her forehead, trailing his lips along the bridge of her nose. 'Thinking about what?'

She reached up and ran her fingers over his dark brows. 'Us, I suppose…'

'Good.' He grinned, 'And you can go on thinking about us, tomorrow, the next week and the week after—the more you think about us the better.'

That meant, she realised, they had a kind of future. The thought filled her with sudden joy, as though she had just been given a reprieve—if only for a few short months.

He pulled her closer, running his hands down her slender back, and she realised their love-making was to begin anew. 'We haven't done very much talking,' he whispered as her arms wound around his neck and she pulled him closer, banishing the thoughts of work and the world in general as desire welled once more and talking was yet again abandoned.

CHAPTER SIX

THE next morning Reece stood behind Holly at the cooker and drew her chestnut hair from her face to kiss her earlobe, running his lips along the smooth curve of her neck.

'Soft centres, as requested,' Holly said, trying not to be distracted by the nibble at her nape as she lifted the eggs from the boiling water and slipped them into the egg-cups. Taking the buttered slices of toast and the honey, she completed the array on the kitchen table with no thanks to the man behind her, clad only in a towel and T-shirt, who undid her chef's apron and slid his hands around her waist.

'Is this how you order from your waitresses in Florida?' she asked with a giggle.

'I haven't seen any waitresses who look like you.'

'Tea?' she murmured.

'Mmm. Lots, please.' He turned her around in his arms and smirked.

'Sugar?'

'All you can spare.'

She quirked an eyebrow. 'Intravenous feed or oral?' she whispered.

They dissolved into laughter. 'Both,' he answered greedily.

'In which case, you'd better leave me with something on so that I can feed you decently.'

'Can I change my mind about what I want for breakfast?'

She pushed him down into the chair. 'Not now I've cooked the eggs.'

She loved to watch him, loved his appetite. Something about America gave men an uninhibited enjoyment of their food. Not that he was American...not quite. The thought brought a sudden swift pain to her heart and she quickly turned her mind to the more practical matters of pouring the tea and buttering more toast.

The man opposite her paused to rub the dark shadow of his jaw and she looked up and smiled. 'Bluebeard,' she teased.

Reece grimaced and growled. Laughing together, they stared into one another's eyes. 'So, what are we going to do?' he said, serious now, leaning his elbows on the table.

'Do?'

'About us.'

She frowned, shrugging. 'I haven't thought that far ahead.'

'You were thinking in bed,' he reminded her.

Colour stole into her cheeks. 'Yes, but on a different level.'

He studied her quietly, then took a breath. 'I plan to go back to the States at Easter. It would be unfair of me to pretend otherwise. If it were left up to me, I would want us to make the most of the time we've got. You're very special to me, Holly.'

'Thank you for being so up-front with me,' she said quietly. 'I'm content with my job and I'm achieving the kind of independence that I value. I wouldn't give it up easily. However, I would like to enjoy what we have, too...for the short time you're here.'

'I see,' he murmured with an obvious hint of relief in his voice. 'Then it's agreed—as we both seem to feel the same way— we'll still see one another? To be honest, I don't think I could stop wanting to see you, even if you said we should stop here.'

Holly smiled. 'You've said some very flattering things.'

'Not flattering—true.' He gazed at her levelly. 'The other thing is do we go public or keep this to ourselves? I don't want to make life difficult for you and you will be the one, after Easter, who has to deal with the situation.'

She toyed with her knife, waiting for the wrench in her stomach to subside. She was not fool enough to believe that this was going to be easy or painless, but she also could not envisage stopping now they had started. 'Perhaps for now we'll keep things to ourselves,' she suggested. 'You can come here whenever you like. The chances are, if you park discreetly, no one will notice.'

He arched an eyebrow. 'We'll give it a shot, then.' He frowned, dropping his eyes to the table. 'And you're sure it will be convenient for me to call—unexpectedly?'

It was a moment or two before she understood, and as his eyes came up to meet hers she knew he was referring to David. And though she understood that they had discovered so much about each other in the last few hours, she was also aware that they had been careful to avoid the most sensitive areas of their lives. With an effort to keep her last meeting with David concise, she explained what had happened at the Harbour Hotel.

'So, it appears I had competition after all?' he said with an effort at humour.

Holly slid her hand towards him across the table. 'No, none whatsoever.'

He closed his hand over hers, drew her to her feet and wrapped her in his arms. 'Oh, Holly, my sweet, I seem to be expecting so much. To suddenly come into your life and demand your undivided attention—' She laid her head on his chest and the penetrating scent of his aftershave filled her senses. 'Tell me what you would like to do today,' he said huskily.

'There's only one thing I want,' she murmured, sliding her hands under his shirt and spreading her fingers across the tight, hard muscle beneath. 'And it involves no more effort than climbing one flight of stairs.'

Reece left her in the early hours of Monday morning, the weekend having been close to perfect for Holly. Her bed seemed oddly lonely without him, and before she fell asleep she buried her face into the pillow, inhaling his aroma. Even her dreams reflected his memory, and when she woke early on Monday morning she gazed at the window for some seconds, her mind trying to separate fact from fiction.

Outside the snow had settled and the weather forecast was for difficulties in all areas of the South-West. As she dressed and breakfasted she wondered if Reece had managed the journey across country to Chartwell, and she found herself barely containing her excitement at the thought of seeing him again.

It was just before she attempted to clear the snow from the Fiesta that Mary Dobson rang. 'Josie's not well,' she explained hesitantly, 'but I didn't want to trouble the doctors in this weather if it turned out to be nothing...'

Holly said she would call but, taking no chances, she phoned the surgery and left word regarding Josie's condition. Having cleared the snow from the Fiesta, she was relieved to hear the faithful chug of her engine, and on her way out of the village she saw that yet again the hardy villagers of North Cornwall were out battling the elements, this time clearing the pavements and paths with shovels.

The gritting lorries had made an early start and the road to the Dobsons' house was clear. But the news on Josie was not so good and the little girl lay in bed, running a fever. 'This time I'm worried,' Mary confided to Holly. 'She hasn't ever been this hot before. Last night she was sick and the aches and pains are back in her arms and legs. Her cheeks and forehead are fevered and her lips are swollen. I've sponged her and given her fluids,' Mary sighed, 'but now she refuses to drink.'

Holly tucked the hot little hand under the sheet just as the doorbell rang. Her heart missed a beat as she heard

Reece's deep voice in the hall below and listened to his long strides as he hurried up the stairs.

'How's my best girl?' He smiled as he came into the room and glanced at Holly, making the kind of eye contact that made her swallow and look guiltily at Mary. But Mary hadn't noticed as she was pulling back the covers for Reece to examine her daughter.

'Let's have a little look, shall we?' He rubbed his big hands together, apologising to Josie for his cold fingers. After examining her, he patted the coverlet gently back around her shoulders.

Downstairs once more, Reece walked slowly through to the lounge. 'It may be a combination of two things—a virus and the anaemia,' he told Mary. 'Bearing this in mind, I would like the paediatrician to keep an eye on her, and the best place to do this is in hospital.'

Mary's expression was resigned. Josie had been in and out of hospital many times, but Holly could not remember when in the last two years Josie had exhibited these confused symptoms.

'I'll pack her bag,' Mary sighed. 'And I'll phone my mother to pick up Joshua from school and let my husband know.'

'Can I do anything to help?' Holly asked.

'No, thanks.' Mary dredged up a smile. 'I know the procedure so well I could do it in my sleep. Will the ambulance be able to get out here in all this snow?'

'Yes, they've cleared the Durnweston road,' Reece assured her. After speaking to the hospital on the telephone and making the necessary arrangements, they left Mary to pack Josie's overnight bag.

Outside the snow had fallen once more in a fine veil and they crunched their way along the path to the cars. Holly luxuriated in the pleasure of looking directly into Reece's eyes as he opened the gate for her. She yearned to reach out and touch him, but somehow she managed not to. The intimacy in his expression was enough for now. Bending his head, he said quietly, 'Are you all right?'

She nodded as their breath curled frostily into the air. 'I'm fine.' She looked up at him. 'It just takes a little getting used to, that's all.'

'The snow?' He smiled, being deliberately obtuse. Then slowly his expression changed as he glanced back at the house. 'I'm really quite concerned about Josie,' he admitted.

'Yes,' Holly agreed, 'and Mary must be, too, although she doesn't comment.'

'Well, hopefully, we'll have caught it in time—whatever it is. I'll feel much happier when she's under the consultant's eagle eye. If it's a false alarm, fine. But if not she'll be in the best place possible. Now...' He frowned thoughtfully, glancing at his watch. 'I've a multiple sclerosis patient to visit, Ken Filler. From his notes, I see you know him.'

Holly nodded. 'Yes, I've called once or twice. Is he ill?'

'No, but he had a fall recently. Nothing broken but there may be some nursing to do in the weeks ahead. Is that enough of an excuse for you to join me there?'

She laughed, but she was only too eager to prolong their time together, no matter what the reason. 'I'll meet you there, if you like.'

He made a soft groan. 'What I would like is to take you in my arms right now and—'

'And have our names carved in local folklore for ever?'

'Spoilsport.' He grinned. 'Drive carefully.'

She nodded and allowed herself one more glance into his warm blue eyes, before they returned to their cars. As she drove she brought Ken Filler to mind, a man who was by trade an accountant. He had developed MS, a disease of the central nervous system, in his early thirties, having been diagnosed after experiencing numbness and a weakness of limbs interspersed with spates of small accidents. Eventually when the disease had progressed, rendering him unable to travel to work, he had moved to Cancreel from Exeter where for the last three years he had worked part time from home.

Vera Filler welcomed them and led them into the large front room. 'Paying bills—that's Ken's trouble,' she joked. 'Gets spots before his eyes when he sees how much I spend on my trips to Exeter.'

Reece responded with a chuckle as he administered the injection which would assist the optic neuritis, or blurred vision, which was linked to the MS condition.

'Even asked for a raise in her housekeeping,' Ken said with a laugh as Reece withdrew the needle and Holly smoothed the pad of cotton wool gently over the entry mark. 'Actually wants to be paid more for spending more! I don't know—women of today, Dr Caine! Might as well let them have the purse-strings and be done with it.'

Reece gave Holly a sly glance and she almost laughed as well.

'Now you're talking!' Vera winked at Holly and, leaving the two men to talk, drew Holly aside to the kitchen. 'I would like you to tell Dr Caine that Ken's vision isn't recovering completely after the injections,' she confided.

'How is his general condition?' Holly enquired.

'Well, he puts on a brave face for my sake but the other day he was slurring his speech so badly I couldn't understand him.'

'In that case, I think it's probably time for a fresh assessment. You're with Dr Peter, aren't you?'

Vera paused. 'Well, Ken is quite happy with his brother.'

'You are aware...' Holly hesitated '...that Dr Caine is acting in a locum capacity?'

Vera shrugged. 'Yes, he did mention it. But he is really

very good with Ken and while he's here we might as well take advantage of the fact.'

Holly nodded, smiling to herself as she reflected that she had also come to the same conclusion, though her interest in Reece was purely selfish and not at all medically orientated!

Reece had finished his examination when they returned and, after saying their farewells, Holly tackled the subject of an assessment as they walked to their cars. Reece nodded as she explained. He was leaning thoughtfully against the Volvo and doodling on the bonnet with his gloved index finger through the snow. 'Ken tells me he hasn't had any occupational therapy sessions lately,' he murmured. 'I'd like to get something organised along those lines but it's only fair I talk to Peter first. Ken is his patient after all.'

Holly was about to respond when she saw he had drawn a heart with an arrow through it and two large initials, R and H. The surprise must have been evident on her face because he reached out to catch her wrist and pulled her gently with him, drawing her behind the two cars where they were not open to view.

'You've got me resorting to childish behaviour,' he said through cold lips. 'The next thing will be scratching your name on my desk at work!'

Holly laughed, feeling like an adolescent herself. 'It was a wonderful weekend, Reece.'

He nodded. 'The trouble is I haven't the least idea when I'm off duty again. I'm certainly on call for the next three nights.'

Holly dug in her pocket and produced the small envelope she had sealed before she'd left home that morning. She blushed as she gave it to him. 'It's the front door key,' she said, unable to prevent her blush from deepening. 'It's for being such a good doodler.'

Over the next two days the snow caused many people to request visits because they could not travel in to the surgery. Holly visited Jonathan who at least conversed, if only minimally, and Ben Sharman still seemed cheerful and did not complain about his catheter. But it was Friday before she saw Reece for any length of time and that was at the Bevans' house when she found Eric Bevan lying on the settee in the front room, looking grey.

'It's nothing much. I'm a bit tired that's all,' he said, but when Mrs Bevan entered and insisted he allow himself to be examined Holly was shocked to discover a puffy and painful redness. She cleaned and dressed the wound as best she could but, having decided an antibiotic was necessary, she telephoned surgery and Bronwyn alerted the duty doctor. Reece arrived within fifteen minutes.

'What happened?' he asked, astonished, as he looked at the wound. 'How long has it been like this?'

'Three or four days,' supplied Eric's wife. 'I thought he'd been a bit off-colour—he just said he was going into the office but now it turns out he gave someone a helping hand on the removal trucks.'

'Which has put you back a bit, I'm afraid,' Reece sighed. 'I'm going to give you an antibiotic. Other than tie you down, I can't think of what else to do. You know you could have caused yourself a real problem.'

'I shan't be doing it again,' Eric Bevan groaned. 'I've learnt my lesson, I can tell you.'

'Do you think he has?' Holly asked as they left.

Reece shrugged. 'He'll be a fool if he doesn't take the warning. This wasn't your official day to visit, I take it?'

Holly shook her head. 'No. But I was passing and I had a kind of...' she shrugged '...impulse to drop in.'

'Clever girl.' He gave her a smile which sent her pulse racing. 'I've missed you,' he said quietly.

'And I've missed you.'

'With luck,' he told her, 'Tim's on call tonight and I can be at your place around sevenish.'

Holly couldn't ignore the flare of excitement in her stomach. 'I'll be waiting with supper,' she promised as they separated, and the day, despite the snow, took on the warm glow of summer.

As she returned to surgery Peter was just leaving. It was barely mid-afternoon but he looked tired and drained as she met him in the car park, about to climb into his specially adapted Audi.

'Oh, hello, Holly.' He gave her a weary smile. 'The snow's clearing a bit, don't you think?'

She nodded, concerned at the many small lines around his eyes and mouth which always revealed the extent of his tiredness. When he did eventually select the correct key he opened the door and eased himself into the car. He sank into the driver's seat, looked up at her and frowned. 'I'm just off. Do you want me for something?'

Holly handed him his case, which he had left on the ground, then she gave him his stick, which he wedged on the back seat but not before she saw him wince. 'No, nothing that won't keep, Peter,' she said lightly. Clearly he was tired and it would serve no purpose to delay him. She was sure he had lost weight lately, quite severely in his face. Was he looking after himself? Pushing himself too much? In both these instances she suspected the answer was yes.

'Off you go,' she said, closing the door. 'And make yourself a cup of tea when you get home. Better still, get Mrs O'Kief to make you a snack of some sort.'

He gazed up at her from the open window, smiling ruefully. 'I'm not so long in the tooth, you know, not to realise we haven't had our usual chat for a couple of weeks. Come back to Chartwell and we'll make ourselves that tea and iron out our patients' problems in the comfort of an armchair. That is, unless you're dashing off somewhere?'

Holly hesitated. 'No, I'm more or less finished now.'

'See you back there, then.'

Holly wondered if she should impose when she knew he was feeling tired but, then, she could at least make sure he did sit down and rest as they talked over the patient queries.

As she climbed into the Fiesta her heart went out to Peter. He wouldn't give in, no matter how tired he was. She was sure that of late, especially, he had been trying to take on board more than he could cope with. She wondered if Reece's dynamism had a rebound effect, causing Peter to drive himself harder and push himself to the boundaries of his strength.

At Chartwell Holly was relieved to have made the decision to accompany him back. In the drawing room he sank into the chair with very little persuasion. Mrs O'Kief made them both a cup of tea and Holly avoided the pleasant lady's gaze as she wondered if Mrs O'Kief had ever considered who, in her absence, had made use of the guest bedroom.

While Peter drank, Holly brought out her notes. After discussing the management of Martha Macreedy, a diabetic, and Kate Barber, a patient with leg ulcers, Holly finally came to Ken Filler.

'I'd be perfectly happy for Reece to see Ken,' he said at Holly's diplomatic suggestion. His face was concerned. 'I'm not quite as active as I'd hoped to be by now. I was hoping to continue on with surgery today.' He gazed up at Holly with a defeated expression. 'I just seemed to run out of steam. God knows, I've let Reece carry all the weight lately. Of course, Reece will have it that it's a bed of roses here.' He laughed genially.

'The pace is incredibly fast in America. He says it doesn't give him time to think, which is, I feel, one of the

main reasons he left England after the Cassandra episode.
With all the memories left here...'

Holly frowned. There was a long silence where Peter
seemed to drift. She had no idea to what he was referring
until finally, leaning back in the chair, he spoke, almost as
though talking to himself.

'It was after Reece's finals,' he sighed. 'Marge was married and living away but Reece expressed interest in a partnership with me. In London he was seeing a girl called
Cassandra. I was surprised when he told me they were going to be married as I'd only met her once or twice and
she didn't strike me as a potential doctor's wife. But she
was a beauty. And Reece was smitten.' Peter's voice
drifted.

'The wedding was arranged here in Cancreel and our
future seemed settled...until the day Reece walked to the
altar and Cassandra decided not to. Needless to say, it was
an experience that changed all our lives... Yes, it certainly
did.'

Almost as if the recalling of such memories had exhausted him, Peter's eyelids fluttered and the teacup, balanced on his knee, slipped. Holly reached out to take it,
supporting Peter's hand with her own.

And it was at that point the door opened and in strode
Reece.

As Holly prepared the supper of oven-baked lasagne she
wondered if Reece would come. Setting candles on the table and laying out the napkins, she recalled the expression
she had seen in his eyes at Chartwell—surprise at discovering her alone with Peter and then a momentary flare of
suspicion. Could he still believe that she and Peter had anything more than a warm regard for each other?

After a brief conversation between the three of them he
had seemed his normal self as he'd walked her to the car.

Still, she had been worrying about it ever since and ached to clear the air.

Her watch said a quarter past seven. When it finally reached half past eight, an hour and a half later than he had suggested, she was convinced Reece would not come. Which was why, when the doorbell rang, she could hardly believe it was him.

'Something smells good,' he said, stepping over the threshold with a wave of frosty air, the collar turned up on his jacket. 'What's all this?' He held her gently as she buried her face in his chest.

'I'm just glad you came,' she whispered.

'Got stuck in the snow for a bit on my last call,' he told her. Prising her away from him, he lifted her chin. 'Did you think I wasn't coming?' He raised a questioning eyebrow. Seeing the answer written on her face, he bent to capture her lips with a deep and urgent kiss.

As he kissed her she agonised over whether or not to bring up the subject of her visit to Chartwell today, the discovery still fresh in her mind of Cassandra, along with her need to reaffirm that she and Peter were only good friends. But it all sounded too much of a cliché and she was frightened he would resent her curiosity about Cassandra, a name which, as she thought of it, sent a sharp dart of jealousy to her heart as she remembered Peter's description of a beauty.

Her problem of communication was resolved as their physical needs overshadowed words. He undressed her there and then, removing her blouse and skirt and running his hands hungrily over her silky underwear with a growing passion which left her breathless for more. Then he lifted her in his arms, carried her upstairs and laid her on her bed, his eyes heavy with need.

'Oh, God, I want you so much,' he whispered, rapidly shedding his own clothes and climbing in beside her. He stretched his body over her, kissing her with renewed demand as she arched against him with wanton abandon.

In those moments Cassandra, Peter, America and all other concerns were forgotten, along with the supper which remained, over-cooked, in the oven downstairs.

CHAPTER SEVEN

REECE had to leave early for a Saturday morning surgery and, having returned for a few hours in the afternoon, was called to a Caesarean delivery in the evening.

He telephoned her that night from Chartwell to say the delivery had been successful but that he had arrived home to find Marge distressed as Peter had had what she'd determined as an angina attack.

Sunday brought no fresh word until the evening when Reece phoned to explain he had not wanted to leave Peter. On Monday morning Holly dressed for work, wondering what hurdle life would present next that might make their meetings more threatened.

By the time she arrived at the surgery Bronwyn and Jo were working together on an open clinic, trying to form some order in a chaotic waiting room. The new practice nurse, Joy, whom Holly had met briefly last week, was already half an hour into her surgery and Kathy, the new receptionist, a more mature woman in her mid-forties, had only a few seconds to introduce herself. Holly discovered that Reece's list was fuller than she had ever seen it and all four doctors were booked solidly until lunchtime, Peter included.

On her way to her first patient her mind reran the events of Friday night and the name, Cassandra. Why had she let Reece down, and had he really left England because of her?

There was also the similarity, too, of her own experience with Martin, though, of course, Reece didn't know about that. She was sure Marge would have kept her confidence and other than the slim chance of Reece having overheard

100

their conversation in the staffroom he knew nothing about Martin and, indeed, had not asked.

Beginning to see that their affair was already showing signs of being more complicated than she'd foreseen, Holly reflected that only a few weeks ago she had been happy with her status as a single career-woman and had thought she had achieved everything she had set out for after Martin. Her friendship with David, she realised, had prevented her from engaging in a relationship with the opposite sex. The unconscious plan had worked well enough until Reece had walked into her life and brought down all her carefully erected defences.

Now, only two months after meeting Reece, she had dispensed with her personal safety valve of David Longshaw and was falling deeper by the day into a torrid, unpredictable and ultimately hopeless affair.

Feeling marginally better for the mental assessment, and quite a deal worse for the outlook it presented, she tried to bring back her thoughts to the priorities of the day.

Her first call was to Martha Macreedy, Peter's patient. Martha was an eighty-six-year-old widow who lived in the village proper in a ground floor flat in sheltered housing accommodation. Martha was a diabetic and a lifetime sufferer of the disease. She needed her insulin injections before breakfast and sometimes became confused, causing the warden of the flats to call in the doctor.

On this occasion Peter had seen the elderly lady last week and had noted that the side-effects of the disease—defective vision, coupled with an inability to concentrate—left her more vulnerable than ever to progressive problems.

This morning, when Holly arrived, the warden looked flustered. 'She's stubborn as a mule,' she declared to Holly. 'Insists she's all right. Won't let me near her.'

'I'll see what I can do.' Holly waited for her knock to be answered and eventually Martha arrived. 'Don't need nursing,' she grumbled in a broad Cornish accent. 'People always interfering.'

'I've just come to check your urine, Mrs Macreedy,' Holly prevaricated, knowing the elderly woman had no quarrel with this procedure as yet. 'You won't mind that, will you?'

Grudgingly her patient allowed her entry. She started Martha talking on the old days and her favourite stories of the fishermen who, in her youth, had abounded on this coast. She soon became lost in her colourful and accurate memories—as opposed to those of the present moment, which were hazy and vague. Holly managed to do the old lady's urinalysis and persuaded her to slip off her slippers in order that her feet could be checked.

'The wimps of today are nothing like the men I used to know,' exclaimed Martha as she rolled off her stocking. 'Now, I've had two husbands, one lost to the sea and one to mining. They were real men—worked all the hours God sends, never was off sick or unemployed, drawing all this money for idling at home. If you ask me, the world needs a good shake-up.'

Holly hid a rueful smile, thinking much the same could be said of Martha's toes. The nails had grown so long they were curling over and there was a nasty bluish tinge to them which looked suspicious. The hazards of infection to lower limbs and the rapidity of gangrene which could so swiftly set in where circulation was deficient were all too common in elderly folk.

'As you can't manage the surgery clinic any more,' Holly decided as she slipped the stocking back on, 'I'm going to ask the chiropodist to call.'

'Don't need one of those,' protested Martha. 'My feet is all right.'

'The toes need attention,' Holly said firmly. 'Don't you think it more sensible to have them looked at before they become troublesome? Or would you prefer me to ask the doctor to visit?'

By the expression on Martha's face, she disliked both ideas, but in the end she agreed to Holly's former suggestion and Holly sat with her for a further ten minutes, trying to gauge more about Martha's maintenance of her diabetes. The need for a diet reduced in carbohydrates and fatty foods seemed to have gone by the board. It was only thanks to the warden that her injections were maintained. It was obvious Martha was becoming confused and forgetful and Holly made a note to suggest reassessment by Peter.

Invariably, elderly folk who could not cope with their own nursing and whose wardens could not be expected to either had only limited choices. Fortunately there were several good nursing homes in Cancreel which might consider taking Martha, the problem being Martha's reluctance to leave her home.

Having spent much longer with Peter's diabetic than she had anticipated, Holly drove next to Kate Barber, an ex-nurse herself, who after retirement had begun to extend her hobby of painting. The single problem which had caused Kate to consult Peter were the varicose leg ulcers which had developed over the past four years.

Kate's home and studio was high on the cliffs outside Cancreel. There was always a warm welcome, despite the fact that the retired nurse effected treatment of her own, rather than keeping up with more modern methods of medicine.

'Come in! Come in! This is a surprise, Holly.' She welcomed Holly with a bright smile and a paint smudged face, already keenly at work on her canvas. Holly's spasmodic visits—when one of Kate's varicose ulcers had been too troublesome for her to cope with—inevitably ended in an enjoyable discussion on village matters.

'Dr Peter wrote a note in my book. He saw your leg last

week and asked me to call in if I was passing your way.' Holly lifted her eyebrows at Kate's bare legs. 'No support stockings?'

'Forgot them, I've been so busy.' Kate grinned, showing her into the L-shaped lounge which was entirely devoted to artist's materials. There was a large oil on the easel, a self-portrait.

'I can see why. It's brilliant, Kate.' The work had captured the vivid expression of Kate's eyes and her still-firm bone structure, despite the fact—or possibly because of it— she was completely silver haired.

'Do you like it?' Kate frowned, wiping her oily hands over her smock, lost in thought. 'It's the first self-portrait I've ever done. I'm a bit lost for sitters so I've had to make do with myself.'

'The likeness is wonderful. But it's your style. Impressionist, isn't it?'

Kate laughed. 'What else, with my crow's feet?'

Holly clucked her tongue. 'You're really very talented. Have you always painted?'

'It's always been a hobby but now I seem to spend all my time in the studio.'

'Which is why you don't come in often enough to see the doctor,' Holly teased gently.

'Oh, I just need a bit of DIY. Heavens, I should know how to manage leg ulcers after a lifetime of teaching others.' Kate sat on a stool and lifted her leg onto a chair for Holly to examine.

'You haven't thought about more surgery?' Holly glanced up to see Kate watching her.

'Only every time you pounce on me and try to drag me in.'

'Well, it would be—'

'The answer to all my problems?' Kate chuckled. 'I've had two lots of stripping and weeks off work, and I'm one of those unfortunate people who keep developing more. No, until it's absolutely vital I'm content to patch myself up— with your help, of course.'

Holly gave a resigned shrug, knowing that the twisted and swollen varicose veins in her patient's legs were as a result of the strain imposed on them by years of upright posture, yet she had never heard a word of complaint from the nurse whose district she had taken over two years ago.

Realising she wasn't about to persuade Kate into surgery just yet, Holly gazed once more at the dressings applied by the older woman. 'Sofra-Tulle?' she asked, frowning.

'I know what you're going to say. Be careful of the danger of contact dermatitis,' Kate sighed. 'But I am careful. And I prefer to use this kind of dressing, despite what might be new on the market. One of the ulcers is a bit raw. I've put a small piece of tulle gras the exact size of the ulcer over it, then a paste bandage.'

Holly nodded as she inspected the site. 'It seems to be working.'

'Did Dr Peter suspect it wasn't?'

Holly glanced up and, smiling wryly, shook her head. 'He knows you well enough to trust your judgement—after twenty years as his DN, he ought to—but all the same he asked me to check.'

Kate smiled. 'Just tell him I'm fine and not to worry. Now, tell me, how is the new boy on the firm?'

Holly knew Kate was referring to Reece. 'Fine,' she said, colouring as she lowered Kate's leg to the floor. 'Now, what about the other one?'

'Not as bad,' answered Kate. 'But go ahead and see for yourself.'

Holly examined the other leg and, though there wasn't much to choose between them, the previous ulcer had begun to heal. Reapplying a fresh dressing, she caught Kate's stare.

'Come on, Holly,' Kate teased. 'Don't keep me in the dark. You know I love to hear all the news.'

Holly grinned. 'In which case you should come in more often and see him for yourself.'

'Oh, I remember him well.' Kate pushed the chair beside her for Holly to sit on. 'He tried to settle down as a GP after his training and I think he would have if it hadn't been for that awful girl—can't remember her name...'

'Cassandra?' Holly put in before she could stop herself.

Kate nodded. 'Yes, that's right, Cassandra. He met her at university, I think. But she dropped out. Used to bring her back home but it was plain to everyone except Reece that she was a city girl and was bored stiff with country life. It was like trying to fit a square peg in a round hole. She would never have settled here. Still, the way she went about ending it knocked him sideways. Next thing was he upped and left for the wide blue yonder.'

Holly sat pensively, her mind once again brought back to the man who seemed to occupy most of her thoughts these days.

'I always liked him,' said Kate. 'Pity, we lost a good doctor there.'

'Yes, he is good,' agreed Holly, 'but temporary, I'm afraid.'

'Which is a shame for Peter and Marge,' Kate sighed. 'With all the changes in the NHS they need someone to chivvy them up. Dear souls they may be but utterly un-businesslike.'

The dressings completed, Holly went out to the bathroom to wash her hands and when she returned Kate was busily back at her easel. Kate turned, studied her and smiled. 'It needs some beautiful young thing to tempt him back to these shores,' she said pointedly.

This time Holly was unable to hide the blush that ran wildly into her cheeks and Kate nodded. 'I thought so,' she said mysteriously. 'I'm glad to see my powers of observation are still strong.'

It was a remark which much to her chagrin, taunted Holly as she drove to the Avises' bungalow, first buying Jonathan's magazine *en route* and several computer ones, too. Was she really so readable when it came to Reece? If Kate, in twenty minutes, had managed to see through her thin veneer, who else had guessed?

Jonathan looked pale when she arrived. Gwen seemed to have lost weight in her face and Doug was struggling to keep his sense of humour going.

'We got him in his wheelchair yesterday,' Doug explained in the kitchen, 'but he's making no effort to move. He's refused to go to the day centre and we can't physically make him, can we?'

Holly gazed through into the bedroom where Jonathan was sitting in bed and Gwen was fussing over him, trying to tempt him into eating breakfast. Holly laid the magazines on the kitchen table.

'Computers?' Doug stared puzzledly at the magazine. Holly paused before she replied. 'Dr Caine thought... well, he wondered if it was possible to encourage Jonathan into taking up a new hobby.' She tailed off, seeing the confusion on the man's face, knowing it was like suggesting a drowning man clutch a twig. But, surprisingly, after a few seconds Doug nodded and shrugged.

'Anything's worth a try, love,' he sighed, 'although the mood he's in at the moment I don't think you'll find him very receptive. His mother's worried sick, to be honest.'

Holly suggested she should give Jonathan a wash and brush-up, and as Gwen had some shopping to do in the village the couple seized the opportunity to go together while Holly remained with Jonathan.

After they had left Holly took the magazines with her into the bedroom. 'Hi, Jonathan,' she called breezily, laying them on the bedside table without referring to them. 'How are you feeling today?'

He looked up with what Holly saw were desolate eyes and her heart twisted for him. He said he was OK but she couldn't get much more out of him. As she sponged and dried him, taking care to apply cream to the sore spots on his spine and heels and finally using the hoist to lift him from the bed and into his wheelchair, she talked about the surgery and news of the village in general. Finally she wheeled him into the lounge. Then there was a knock at the door and Holly hurried to answer it.

'Thought I might find you here.' Reece grinned and, walking in, narrowed his eyes. 'Jonathan up?'

She nodded. 'In the lounge. Gwen and Doug are shopping. I've given him the magazines,' she whispered softly.

To her surprise Reece caught her by the waist and, throwing a glance to see if they were unobserved, bent to brush his lips swiftly over hers. 'My clever girl,' he muttered, and with another firmer tug kissed her again, only letting her go when they heard Jonathan's movement.

'Hi, there, Jonathan!' Reece called, and rolled his eyes as he took off his coat and hung it on the hall-stand.

In the lounge Reece sat beside Jonathan and glanced casually at the magazines. Holly went to make a hot drink for everyone and she saw Gwen had left sandwiches. She took them back with her, hoping to persuade Jonathan to eat too. When she arrived back in the room Jonathan was frowning at the magazine on his lap.

Reece said, 'Jonathan's been telling me a bit about computers.' He looked at her with innocent blue eyes.

Jonathan shrugged. 'I've been watching the technology programmes on TV, that's all.'

'Oh,' said Holly. 'I'm afraid I don't understand all the techno-language.'

'It's easy enough,' Jonathan said dismissively and began

to turn the pages. She was surprised when he translated the jargon and Reece, suitably impressed, managed to keep the conversation going for a good fifteen minutes afterwards.

'I think I'll go back to bed now,' Jonathan said eventually, and that was as much as they got out of him until Gwen and Doug returned.

'We'll keep up the pressure,' Reece told her when they left. 'At least we've made a start.'

The positive note evaporated when on their return to the surgery they met Mary Dobson, looking pale and upset.

'Josie's very poorly,' she explained. 'We're at the hospital nearly all of the time. One of us there, one of us with Josh. They've told us it's a severe infection, the worst sickle-cell crisis she's ever had. They're giving her antibiotics and analgesics, but the control of the pain is really a problem. It's so awful to see her...' Mary's face crumpled and Holly slid an arm around her shoulders and gave her a gentle hug.

'Come in,' Reece suggested gently, 'and tell us all about it.'

They led Mary back into the surgery and in Reece's room Mary sat slowly in a chair and Holly drew one up beside her as Reece took another. Mary blew her nose and struggled to regain her composure. Finally she took a breath and lifted her head. 'The doctor told us today,' she explained, 'that Josie's blood vessels are clogged. This causes something called an-an—'

'Anoxia,' said Reece, nodding. 'Basically it's a lack of oxygen.'

'Josie's disease is inherited from her parents and her red blood cells contain an abnormal haemoglobin,' Mary said shakily. 'It distorts the blood cells into sickle shapes, doesn't it?' Reece nodded and Mary swallowed. 'But what we didn't understand was that the disease is resistant to an infection which causes a kind of malaria. And they think Josie's got this—this kind of related fever.'

Reece paused. 'It can be treated,' he said gently. 'They will do everything possible to help her recover, Mary.'

'We knew it would be difficult…' Mary began to weep '…but we didn't know how difficult. We love her so much. Sh-she's such a brave little girl.'

'Her spirit will help her,' Holly murmured as a lump grew in her throat at the thought of the tiny slip of a girl who had always shown such bravery in the face of her disease.

'When we lived in London,' continued Mary, wiping her eyes, 'the hospital had other children with the same complaint but here Josie is the only one. The same as she is the only black child at her new school. It makes us wonder if we did the right thing, bringing her away from the city. We thought it would be a f-fresh start, with the sea and the beach, but now…'

'Of course you did the right thing,' Reece said immediately. 'Cornwall is a wonderful place to live and when Josie's well you'll be able to take her to the sea and the beach and enjoy it all, as you planned. You must keep thinking positively for Graham's and Josh's sake as well as Josie's—keep remembering all the qualities you wanted to enrich your lives with.'

Mary nodded, giving a deep sigh. She looked up, her eyes red and puffy, but she managed a smile. 'Yes, yes. You're both very kind… It's good to have someone to speak to. I don't like to worry Graham.'

'We're here whenever you want us,' Reece said encouragingly. 'Or at the end of the telephone line.'

'I know. Thank you.' Mary stood, pulling back her shoulders, and Reece escorted her through to Reception where Holly watched him talk to Mary for a few moments more.

Wishing there was something more constructive she could have done to help, Holly walked back to Alison's desk and sat down. She was well aware that sickle-cell crises like this could result in damage to the vital organs. Should the blood flow be impaired, the heart and kidneys were at risk. So far Josie had evaded this threat, but now it seemed the little girl was in real danger.

Without hearing Reece re-enter the room and cross towards her, Holly chewed at her lip with a frown.

'Don't look so worried,' Reece said in a soft voice. She jumped as she looked up at him, her expression changing swiftly to apprehension.

'But it is serious, isn't it?' she asked hesitantly.

He nodded, going to the window to stare out, his hands thrust deeply into his pockets. 'I phoned Josie's consultant this morning before Mary came in. He told me they are very concerned. Some of Josie's sickle cells have been removed from the circulation, which has led to the anaemia. They're doing all they can, but over the years there's proved to be no one really satisfactory treatment. The obvious danger is kidney and heart failure.

'If it's kidney an intravenous drip of blood or plasma is normally used with a diuretic drug—that's all that's needed to restore function—but with sickle-cell, because of the nature of the disease, it's not so straightforward. All I can say is that Josie is a born little fighter. And I think from Mary's point of view she'll feel stronger now, having put her fears into words.'

Holly remained silent, lost in thought, until suddenly she felt the warm touch of his hand on her shoulder. She looked up to see him, staring down at her.

'Twenty-two days left,' he said, lifting an eyebrow.

Her heart took an enormous leap. 'Left for what?'

'To Christmas,' he chuckled. 'What else?'

'Oh, is it?' She laughed quickly, annoyed with herself

for the confusion in her brain as she'd imagined he was referring to the time they had left with each other—an obsession which seemed to be filling her mind lately, causing her to make idiotic mistakes such as this.

'Have you thought of what to buy me yet? he asked in a serious voice.

This time she laughed. 'No, but I have the feeling you're going to make a suggestion.'

'Yes,' he said huskily, drawing her to her feet, 'I want more of this.' Despite the sound of footsteps beyond the door, he kissed her until she was breathless, only breaking apart as Kathy walked into the room.

The thaw and December's practice meeting came on the same day, Monday, nearly a week later. Holly was present at the meeting, along with all the staff. First on the agenda was the streamlining of reception and office procedure.

'An occasional secretary isn't sufficient,' Reece started off. 'We need a practice manager who can set up more efficient surgeries, eradicate the confusion of on-call days and weekends and generally solve practice problems.'

'I would have thought three reception staff and a part-time secretary were enough,' Peter said with a frown. 'Don't you think a practice manager is going a little O.T.T.?'

Reece shook his head. 'Very few practices operate without them, Peter, either here in England or abroad. You and Marge have always coped with the finer details, but with increasing pressures it's essential. Before I leave I would like to see you fully up and running.'

Peter's face dropped.

Reece went on, 'By pressures I refer to the enlargement of our area, Peter. I see by my figures our lists have grown over the last year and, hopefully, fully staffed, we should provide a better service to meet it.'

'We're certainly much busier,' agreed Marge, glancing at Peter.

'And I can say from experience,' said Alison bluntly, 'until Joy stepped in to help me I couldn't provide the range of clinics we're now doing between us. In fact, I was thinking of packing in nursing altogether because I'd got so swamped here and at home. Then Dr Caine suggested this new arrangement with Joy and it's perfect.'

'Thank you, Alison,' said Reece, clearing his throat at the unexpected support. 'I think the key word here is expansion. We're broadening our horizons, as is society in general—and the NHS. The hospitals discovered long ago how important good management is. I think we've got to follow suit.'

'Also, if we're expanding at such a rate,' Tim said thoughtfully, 'then wouldn't it be sensible to think about a replacement for you, Reece? GPs aren't so easy to find these days. And in this part of the country...' He shrugged, pausing a moment. 'What I'm saying is when you return to America we shall have outgrown ourselves to the point where we shall need a fourth doctor—unless anyone has any other ideas?'

Silence descended on the room. Holly held her breath and waited for his reply, wondering irrationally if Reece's answer might leave room for hope. But her heart sank the moment he spoke.

'Yes, you're right, Tim. The three of you will have to decide what it is you want of a partner—a male or female replacement, age and so forth and whether you have any personal or professional criteria to be met. Perhaps you should give the matter some thought over Christmas and at January's meeting throw in suggestions.'

Holly made a deliberate effort to loosen her clenched hands. She had known all along that he was leaving so why this reaction now? She had wanted their affair to continue—she had agreed without hesitation. He had never in any way misled her as to his intentions so why was she hoping for a miracle now?

'I've a patient who has just moved to Cancreel,' said Marge after a while, thankfully breaking the deepening gloom into which the room seemed to have fallen. 'She was with a Devon practice for about ten years in a secretarial capacity but she's a very efficient and organised person. She mentioned she was looking for work. Perhaps she might be interested in the practice manager's post.'

'Excellent,' said Reece. 'If she can give us a CV and come in for interview...?'

'I'll telephone her,' Marge said.

'And I'm happy to look for a replacement,' offered Tim. 'I'll contact one or two colleagues over the holiday.'

'Good. Thanks, Tim.' Reece did not meet Holly's gaze and her breath stilled as his blue eyes circled the room. Then Alison and Joy explained their intention to begin stress-related clinics for patients most vulnerable to anxiety, and this idea drew all four doctors into fresh enthusiasm.

Trying hard to engender some enthusiasm too, Holly finally devoted a few minutes to the patients on her daily rounds with whom all the doctors were familiar. Martha Macreedy and Ken Filler were both earmarked for fresh assessment and everyone had concerns for little Josie in hospital.

Then Peter, who related to Jonathan's disability problems, asked for an update on him. Holly was hesitant, at last catching Reece's glance. She began to explain the pattern of his depression and the idea of a new hobby. Peter, who had been the quietest during the meeting, suddenly perked up.

'Would you like me to slip along and see him?' he suggested. 'Not that I'll be able to do much, but I might be able to give him some encouragement. Technology quite takes my fancy, too.'

Holly was delighted to agree and Reece echoed his support. Their eyes met afterwards with a flicker of shared understanding, though each of them was swift to look away.

By the time the meeting was over darkness had fallen. Everyone buttoned up their coats to meet the cold night air. Reece caught up with Holly as she walked to the door. 'I'm calling in to see Ben Sharman,' he told her. 'Bronwyn took a call from him this afternoon. He said there was no urgency and tomorrow would do but I thought I'd pop out there tonight. I know you've seen him since my last visit. How did he seem?'

Holly shrugged. 'Quite happy, surprisingly. He seems to have got used to the catheter. And I think I've started him thinking along the lines of investigations.'

'That's good news.' Reece's blue eyes were fired with enthusiasm. 'Perhaps he wants to talk about it—would you like to come with me?'

'Wild horses wouldn't keep me away.' Forgetting herself for a moment, she gazed longingly at the full, smiling mouth and her mind flew back over the last week to their snatched and passionate meetings.

She had never known such freedom of physical and emotional energy and her heart told her that the laws of common sense had long ceased to apply to their relationship, nor would she want to change a second of the time she spent with him.

As she joined him in the Volvo she leaned back in the comfortable and familiar seat, content to let the pleasure of just being with him wash over her. There was little sign left of the snow and the car glided swiftly through the night. She listened to the smooth, strong tones of Reece's voice as he talked, and she knew that someone very special had been sent into her life. She determined once again to make the most of every moment.

There were no lights showing in Ben's cottage as they drove into the pebble driveway. They clambered from the car as a fresh sea breeze swept over the coastline and shook the little wicket fence. All the windows were in darkness, and as they approached the door the familiar sound of Ben's radio was noticeably absent.

They knocked and waited, but received no response. 'Someone must be at home,' Reece muttered, and tried the door.

It opened. The air was still as they walked inside and the house was icy cold. Holly's fingers fumbled for a light switch. When she found it Reece headed upstairs, leaping them two at a time. She listened to his footsteps across the bare boards as she wandered around the deserted living room, the empty downstairs bedroom and finally the kitchen. The old white sink was clear of dishes, the wooden chairs neatly pushed under the table. On the blue and white check oilcloth she saw an envelope.

Reece came into the kitchen and she handed it to him. 'It's for you.'

He took it and slowly slid a finger under the seal, his forehead creasing as he silently read the few lines. When he looked up he shook his head, his expression shuttered for a few moments until finally he passed her the note.

Dr Caine, Thank you for calling. I would like you to know I'm grateful for all you and your young lady have done. But I'm tired now and I'm going down to the sea. I have left a letter for the solicitor. Please see he receives it. Yours in appreciation, Benjamin Sharman.

CHAPTER EIGHT

HOLLY read through the letter again, trying to find some note of hope, but the message was dreadfully final. A large arm went around her shoulders as she put a hand to her mouth, and after a moment Reece squeezed her shoulder. 'I'd better alert the police. Then perhaps I'll take a flashlight and go to the beach. The chances are he'll have taken the cliff path. Our only hope might be that he didn't have enough strength to make it.'

Holly nodded. 'Yes, that's a possibility, I suppose.' But she had the instinctive feeling that everything they now did would be a pure formality. The finality of the note indicated that Ben would have struggled to reach the beach with his last breath.

When Reece came back into the kitchen she had composed herself. 'I'll take the flashlight from my boot,' he told her. 'I shouldn't be long.'

'I want to come with you.' Holly's grey eyes were determined. 'If...if there is any chance I may be of some help.'

There was a brief hesitation before he nodded, and together they left the cottage, taking the flashlight. The darkness enveloped them immediately as they crossed the narrow lane which led to the cliff path. Reece pointed the torch at the wooden signpost which directed tourists to the beach and a fresh wave of salt air blew into their faces as they followed the track.

Reece shone the flashlight onto all the grassy dunes and into any sandy nooks and crannies which might shelter a human being, but when they came to the steep gradient which led down to the sea the path was deserted.

In summer the walk would have meant a sunny day's outing, a peaceful trip to the beach for the odd tourist, but now, in the depths of winter, the path looked desolate and Holly shivered in the squall which blew around them as they came closer to the sea.

If they had expected to find Ben on the route down it was only because they had been unable to grasp that he would seriously contemplate taking his own life. But after they'd reached the sea-front and had shone the light as far as they could in each direction Reece shook his head. 'We'll walk two hundred yards both ways,' he shouted against the wind. 'Are you OK?'

She nodded as she hunched her shoulders and pulled her warm winter coat closer around her, turning up the collar to keep out the wind. The sea powered in savagely and huge white breakers crashed along the shore, one after another, in the pitch blackness. Taking her hand, he drew her beside him and together they searched westwards and then retraced their steps eastwards. Finally coming back to where they had begun, Reece pointed to the path. 'Let's walk back up and meet the police. Perhaps they'll make an extended search.'

The journey uphill was broken by the shadowy figures of policemen in the distance, also equipped with flashlights which bobbed eerily in the distance. When they converged, Reece directed them to the path they had followed and explained the area they had covered. Back at the cottage two patrol cars were parked behind the Volvo and Fiesta, and an ambulance had made its way up to the front door.

There was nothing anyone could do now, Holly realised, but wait.

It was six days before Christmas, a bright, cold Thursday, just as Josie Dobson began to show the first signs of recovery in hospital, that the news of Ben came in. Holly had just arrived at surgery, hoping to catch Marge before she left for her visits, and she was passing the details of a diabetic visit to her when Reece walked into the office.

'The police have telephoned,' he said simply. 'A body has been discovered on a beach two miles along the coast. They've asked me to make a formal identification. As far as I can gather by the description they gave me, it sounds as though it could be Ben.'

Holly felt her legs go weak and she had to force herself not to give in to the temptation of sinking into the chair. The news was not unexpected, although now it had come it was a terrible shock. What was so upsetting was that Ben had seemed to be adjusting to his problems and she'd honestly thought she'd convinced him to go in for further investigations. Reece had comforted her by saying that he thought Ben had never had any intention of returning to hospital and he'd most probably been planning something else while seeming to be more malleable to her suggestions.

'I should only be away for the morning,' Reece told them. 'Could I ask you and Tim to share my list, Marge?'

'Of course. I'll go and sort it out with Bronwyn and Kathy now.' Marge walked from the room, stopping briefly to lay her hand on her brother's arm.

'Is there anything I can do?' Holly asked, after Marge had left them.

'At the moment, nothing. There's no family to inform or relations, as far as we know—unless someone turns up out of the blue.'

'Do you think...?' Holly asked in a faint voice. 'Do you think Ben killed himself because he was lonely?'

'I think he was alone, but not lonely,' Reece told her quietly. 'When his illness started I imagine he foresaw a time when he wouldn't be able to retain control of his life.

He hated the hospital environment and I'm quite sure nothing on God's earth would have persuaded him to go back into one. So he made his decision and left this mortal coil on his own terms.'

'But the thought of all that sea and one tiny, helpless individual—'

'It was his wish,' Reece interrupted, crossing the room to slide an arm around her shoulders and give her a little shake. 'His choice. And the last thing he would have wanted was for you to torture yourself over it. Now, can I leave you, without worrying you're going to brood?'

Holly nodded, looking up into his concerned face. 'Yes, I'll be all right.'

'That's my girl. I shouldn't be more than a couple of hours, but if anyone needs me I'll have the mobile.' He gave her shoulder one last squeeze before he picked up his case and walked to the door to attend to his sombre duty.

Holly went on to make several visits during the morning to her elderly patients who needed attention first thing. A new diabetic who needed assessment was first on her list, then a pensioner who had psoriasis, an unsightly and uncomfortable rash which necessitated a steroid cream.

Refusing to allow her mind to dwell on Ben, she finally visited an elderly man with emphysema, a lung condition which caused him increasing shortness of breath. As he persisted in smoking, the case was even more frustrating, but despite this Holly encouraged frequent examinations and checked he was using his bronchodilator correctly.

When she finally arrived in mid-afternoon at the Avis household the physiotherapist's car was parked in the drive. When she knocked, Gwen opened the door with a ready smile.

'Holly! You're just in time to catch Margaret.'

'How is the physio coming along?' Holly took off her coat and accepted the offer of a cup of tea.

'Since Dr Peter's visit, a little better. His call was un-official—or so he told Jonathan—but the two of them had a long chat and as a result he's co-operating with Margaret now.'

Just as Gwen finished speaking Margaret Johnson, the physiotherapist, appeared. 'Hi, Holly,' she said, reaching for her coat on the hall-stand. 'We've had a constructive hour, haven't we, Gwen?'

Gwen nodded, her eyes going to Holly. 'I'm just afraid it won't continue. He's been in such a depression recently.'

'Well, yes, there's always that chance,' Margaret agreed candidly as she pulled on her coat, 'but we've taken a step forward today and we'll try to maintain it.'

Margaret departed and Holly went into the lounge where Jonathan was dressed and sitting in his wheelchair. His hair was neatly combed and, rather than watching the television, he was doing the arm exercises Margaret had taught him. He told Holly he was able to use his fingers to grasp more firmly and, using his hands to move the wheelchair, Holly saw him for the first time make a real effort to use his upper body.

When she finally returned to surgery her spirits, which had lifted while she was with Jonathan, sank again when she saw the Volvo parked on the hill. In the surgery Bronwyn was at the desk and beckoned her over. 'Dr Caine said he'd like to have a word,' she murmured in a lowered tone. 'I've taken him in a cup of tea. Would you like one?'

'No, thanks.' Holy smiled gratefully. 'I'll go in now if he's not busy.'

Bronwyn nodded and Holly went along to his room. He was sitting at his desk, head bent, his dark hair catching the light from the window and his broad shoulders hunched in concentration. At first he didn't hear her, even though she had tapped before going in. When he lifted his gaze she could see the sadness clouding his eyes and knew immediately before he spoke the result of his morning's trip.

He gestured to her to sit and she occupied the patient's chair. 'It was Ben, wasn't it?' she said, on a resigned sigh.

He nodded, his jaw tightening as he looked at her. 'The tide had taken him into a cove further down the coast and not out to sea. I suppose we should be grateful we're not left in doubt and he can have a proper burial. I informed his solicitor of my identification and all the legal aspects, including the funeral for which Ben had provided, will be taken care of.'

Holly nodded slowly. 'When will the funeral be, do you think—before Christmas?'

Reece looked doubtful. 'Because of the circumstances things may take longer. There will have to be a post-mortem, of course.'

'Then it's a blessing there are no relatives,' Holly said, clearing her throat. 'Having something like that hanging over one's head throughout Christmas…' She could read the expression in his eyes and knew that, despite his outer calm, he was feeling the loss deeply, his mind turning over the events which had led to Ben's suicide. Though neither of them referred to it, they had become closer to Ben than anyone else over the last few months.

He sat back in his chair and with an abrupt smile nodded to the rather dog-eared set of records in front of him which Holly recognised. 'We've a little good news in Josie's direction,' he told her. 'She's apparently responding to treatment, and as I'm not on call this evening I thought about making a visit. I phoned Mary and she's gone this afternoon, leaving tonight free. How do you feel about a trip over to Durnweston?'

'Oh, yes,' Holly agreed instantly. 'I'd love to.'

'We should allow three quarters of an hour to get there.

My surgery ends at five-thirty, and if I change here and come to pick you up immediately we should make it at the latest by half six. We can stop somewhere afterwards for a bite to eat, if you like.'

She nodded slowly, her heart beating harder with unashamed excitement. 'I'll be ready.'

For a simple hospital visit, Holly realised she was making as much of an effort with her appearance as she would have for a date, but the opportunities to actually go out with Reece since their day at Penwarrell had been few and far between. Taking extra care with her hair, she washed it and dried it carefully into a shining bob. Today she'd arrived home at four and had treated herself to a soak in a hot bath with natural oils. After completing her hair, she had chosen a new midi-length skirt and warm grey sweater from the assortment of outfits she had laid carefully over the bed.

She was tall enough to take long skirts and pumps if she chose but this evening she opted for small-heeled fashion shoes, and with a rare enjoyment she slid on soft cream silk underwear, fragile misty stockings with exquisite lacy tops and a suspender belt which could be termed nothing but a little bit of fun. When her outfit was complete she twirled in front of the mirror, telling herself that the effect she had taken so much trouble to achieve was for Josie's benefit too.

When she thought of a whole evening and possibly a night with Reece she trembled a little. Simple pleasures were like gold dust and she had come to realise how grateful she was for a job in which she could be close to him and also, despite their differences of opinion—as had happened with regard to Jonathan and Ben—in the early stages of their relationship, she now knew that she had come to understand and respect his methods of working and, hopefully, the same could be said of his feeling towards her.

No doubt there would always be a difference of opinion where patients were concerned. Reece was dynamic and decisive. She, on the other hand, motivated her patients with less energy and was reticent about pushing too hard when a person resisted, a philosophy which had always blended with Peter's and Marge's techniques. But life changed, was always changing. And, as Reece had proved in such a short time, changes in the system were not to be feared but could effectively improve working practice, as had happened over the last few months at the surgery.

Then, just before Reece was due to arrive, Holly sank to the bed, her heart twisting with a sudden arrow of pain. What was she thinking of? There she went again, imagining he was part of her life—her future. There would never be the opportunity to exchange opinions or methods or techniques, not after Easter. It was hard now to think she had ever wanted her life as it had been. Alone and independent she had protected herself against feeling, against hurting again after Martin and, probably, after the loss of her father.

But these were the deep waters of the psyche. All she knew was she had been content with her life before Reece came into it. Not happy, but content with her lot. Perhaps she truly had not wanted a commitment then—perhaps she had sealed herself off effectively from involvement. But now...now so much had changed.

Reece was dressed in jeans and a deep blue sweater when he arrived, a change of clothes he kept at work and which had come in useful this evening. He looked tall and sexy and his smile was wonderful to see as she opened the door before he was halfway up the path.

His eyes widened in admiration as he came closer and saw her in the glow which spilled out from the open doorway into the winter's evening. She had a mental picture of his expression then—one she committed to memory as his silhouette moved towards her, outlined by the bright lights

of the houses opposite and the twinkling of the coloured
stars on Christmas trees.

'You look beautiful,' he said, as she stood aside to let
him in and closed the door. They stood in the silence of
the small, warm hall and he took her in his arms, holding
her so tightly she hardly heard him mutter, 'I wish we
weren't going out now.'

'Me, too,' she admitted.

'What a day,' he groaned. Closing his eyes, he drew her
into his hard, warm chest and leaned his chin against her
head. 'Although I'm looking forward to seeing Josie, I can't
tell you how much I just want to curl up in your bed and
hold you and have you all to myself.'

A lump grew in her throat of such proportions she
couldn't speak and she was glad her face lay against his
chest and that he couldn't see the sudden and irrational tiny
tears spill over her cheeks. Perhaps it was the after-effects
of Ben, or her silly bout of brooding upstairs, or perhaps it
was his deep and husky voice which travelled so powerfully
through his body and symbolised to her the rock on which
she had begun to lean that made her want to cry.

After she'd luxuriated in his arms she swallowed her
emotion and, slipping out of his arms, made a pretext of
finding her coat. She took her time, running upstairs and
making a lot of unnecessary noise, for she knew when she
returned to face him that her lips would be smiling and he
would never know what ridiculous thoughts had gone
through her mind.

A few minutes later Reece nodded to a large, fleecy,
white toy polar bear, sitting on the back seat of the Volvo
with a scarlet ribbon tied around its neck. He raised dark
eyebrows as he started the engine. 'I hadn't a clue what to
bring but I thought it was the type of thing she could
cuddle.'

'It's beautiful!' Holly picked it up and rubbed her face into the soft fur. 'She'll love it. Where did you find it?'

'At the newsagents in the village, would you believe? They've a section for almost everything imaginable, especially Christmas gifts. I bought a CD for Josh, too, some band the girl recommended—haven't a clue who they are, but she said they're a favourite with all the kids.'

Holly was once again touched by his thoughtfulness, and even more so when, on their arrival at the hospital, he openly slid an arm around her waist as they walked to the children's ward, nuzzling her ear affectionately as he bent to whisper, 'You must be absolutely famished. We'll stay for just half an hour and then I'll take you somewhere and feed you.'

The fact that he didn't seem to worry about who saw them caused her a wave of anxiety. Was it a good sign or a bad one? Did he really not worry who knew of their affair? In which case he must be happy to be seen with her—or was it that out of Cancreel he simply felt free to show his affection?

He insisted on holding her hand as they walked into the ward, which was decorated with sparkling, glittery decorations and a huge Christmas tree just inside the doors. It was visiting time and the beds were surrounded by parents of the children. A few pyjama-clad little bodies manoeuvred to and from the day room where a television blared out carols.

Neither of them had foreseen the possibility that Josie would be waiting anxiously for them, sitting on her bed with her eyes glued to the ward door, and it was something of a shock as she threw her arms around Holly's neck and hugged her.

'Hey! Save some for me!' Reece's deep chuckle was lost in Josie's cries of delight as she spotted the polar bear. She held it at arm's length, her lovely dark eyes wide in delight.

'I've got one at home,' Josie told them as they settled

her back into bed, with the bear tucked tightly in her arms, 'but he's got no eyes.'

Reece perched on the foot of the bed, winding one long leg around the other, and Holly took the chair. 'You'll have to give this one a name,' he said with a grin. 'We can't just keep calling him Bear.'

Josie giggled and stuck a thumb in her mouth. 'I like Bear.' But suddenly she was silent. 'Will they let me into school if I'm better?'

Holly squeezed her hand. 'Of course they will, poppet. Why ever shouldn't they?'

'Because they've all started already and I won't know what to do.'

Reece cast a glance at Holly. Gently he leaned forward and stroked Bear. 'When I was just a little older than you I had to have my tonsils out. I had started a new school, too, but I soon caught up. And I made a friend who told me everything I'd missed. It was pretty good fun.'

'Will I make a friend?' The little thumb dragged over trembling lips.

'Guaranteed.' Reece smiled.

Holly listened to him as he expounded on this theme, and Josie was charmed and distracted, her dark eyes going over Reece's handsome face as he talked. One day, she thought with a pang, he would make a wonderful father. Cassandra never knew what she had missed.

Quite suddenly Holly realised he had stopped talking and was leaning across to tuck both Bear and Josie under the sheet. Josie's thick black eyelashes fluttered sleepily to her cheek and she turned her head into the pillow.

'Out like a light,' he whispered. Putting his lips against Holly's ear, he added, 'I'm glad my company doesn't have the same effect on you.'

'No, quite the opposite,' she sighed. She slipped her hand through his arm, taking comfort from the smile which

opened his soft, moist lips and the expression of promise
in his eyes which drained the strength from her legs.

Eventually, hand in hand, they slipped from the ward,
and on the drive homeward she snuggled against him, savouring the hours that lay before them.

'Happy?' he whispered in the darkness.

'Very,' she said softly, and knew that she would never
be able to tell him quite how her perception of happiness
had changed in the time she had known him.

This night, Holly thought, is going to be special.

And it was. Perhaps because of the sharp contrast between Ben and Josie and the inevitable nostalgia created by
this time of the year she felt closer to Reece than she had
ever done. When they saw the lights of the True Lovers'
Knot on the way home from Durnweston it seemed appropriate to park the car in the tiny car park and stand below
the swinging sign and stare up at it, their arms linked
around each other's waists and their collars pulled up to
their chins.

'This must be for us,' he said, as he looked down and
gently brushed his lips over her hair. He added softly,
'Hungry?'

She nodded. 'But not especially for food.'

'Me, too.' He rubbed her arm, pulling her closer. 'But
we do have to eat. Come on, let's get into the warm.'

It was an enchanting little pub with only a few locals in
the lounge bar. There was a golden glow over the green
tub chairs and round wooden tables. The Christmas tree was
balanced on the bar and bore the stencilled names on silver
balls of each customer who had given to its specified charity. From the bar next door came laughter and the smell of
pipe smoke and keg beer pervaded even the pleasant aroma
of a faint cooking.

They ordered scampi in the basket and drank low-alcohol

lager, although Reece drank little of his, concentrating on his food. When they had finished, Holly shifted against him on the comfortable corner bench seat and leaned into his crooked arm, which stretched behind her head on the seat, watching the bar slowly fill up.

For a fleeting, unreasonable moment she wondered if the time was right to tempt providence. She had wondered if she should try to explain about Martin and whether, in turn, Reece would speak of Cassandra. Since Peter had mentioned her, Holly had sometimes found herself speculating, only to rein in her curiosity as the moment never seemed right to ask Reece. If she felt this way then, by the same token, did Reece feel much the same way regarding Martin? Or was he content, bearing in mind their temporary arrangement, to leave the past undisturbed?

In the end, once again, she decided against it. Reece seemed happy to run his fingers through her hair and occasionally comment on the men playing shove-halfpenny, their expertise in no doubt as they put palm against board to propel the coins towards their targets.

Holly captured the intimate scenes in her mind—a profile here, a gesture there, a smell, a scent, a voice, a colour. She catalogued it all, knowing one day she would look back on these memories and relive them. This was her Christmas in all its simplicity, her own special time of intimate and immeasurable pleasure.

A pleasure to be deliciously extended as they drove home and parked the Volvo, walking the few yards to her house. Her Christmas tree, smaller even than the pub's, sparkled through her window and she felt a stab of pride as she unlocked the front door and drew Reece in after her, only letting go of his hand as he turned her to face him, brushed the hair from her face and cupped her head in his hands.

'I thought we'd never make it,' he sighed. 'You look so

lovely this evening. I was watching you in the pub and I wondered how I could be so lucky.'

'Watching me?'

'I've eyes in the side and back of my head when it comes to you.'

She laughed. 'I can't see them. Only this...' She smoothed her fingers up and into the thick black hair, which grew down over his collar, and teased the rims of his ears by folding his hair behind them and tugging gently, laying her fingers over the lobes and rubbing.

'That's wonderful,' he whispered, arching his neck. 'I'm afraid to move in case you stop.'

'I shan't stop. But we can't stand here all night. And it would be far easier to massage them if you were horizontal.'

'As long as you're horizontal too, I can't think of a single objection.'

Holly realised they had both been pacing themselves throughout the evening, savouring what was to come and what could not be interrupted. Tim was on call, the answerphone was turned on downstairs and the door was solidly bolted. The night was theirs.

If she had imagined that their love-making had reached its zenith before, tonight she found she had been mistaken. There was nothing less than perfection in the way he touched her, aroused her and made her wait patiently as he brought her to a slow and shuddering awareness of her own needs, wrenching a cry from her throat as his hands completed their exotic path over every inch of her body into warm and moist valleys of skin and smooth, sleek hills of proud bone covered by tiny, throbbing blue veins of warm, highly charged blood.

She thought she would cry out again and tried by force of will to moderate her ecstasy. Falling desperately short as another half sob, half entreaty strained from her lungs, he entered her and with the consummate ease of a skilful lover set free at last the ache imprisoned inside her.

Moments later she lay in his arms, guiltily aware of her selfishness. Turning to gaze into the satiated blue eyes which told her that he, too, was fulfilled, she let herself be cuddled against him, bound invisibly by the bonds of their perfect love-making.

CHAPTER NINE

Two separate incidents helped to make Christmas a total disaster. The first was that Reece had opted for Christmas Eve as his free day, volunteering for the on-call duty over Christmas Day and Boxing Day. The second was the arrival of Holly's mother and stepfather the night before Christmas Eve.

Holly was to reflect later that the confusion had probably been precipitated entirely by her for she had made innumerable excuses not to stay over at the hotel this year, a ritual she had rarely missed, and she'd had no idea that her mother and Brendan would make the journey to see her.

'It's because of David, isn't it?' Sara Lewis, chic and dark-haired, with her daughter's large grey eyes, stood in the kitchen, making wild guesses as to why Holly had refused their invitation.

Holly was preoccupied. Reece, who had arrived at almost the same time as her parents, was sitting with Brendan in the other room, blissfully unaware of the turn of events which Holly feared was unfolding.

Brendan and her mother had arrived at five just as Holly had driven up. She'd hardly believed her eyes as the next to arrive had been Reece, who, realising too late that she'd had company, had parked the Volvo directly behind her parents' BMW and had been formally introduced as Dr Caine.

Holly had planned to devote the next twenty-four hours to indolent enjoyment with Reece as they had both managed to reserve Christmas Eve for themselves, but now that prospect was beginning to look increasingly doubtful.

'No, Mother,' Holly said, suddenly hearing what her anxious parent had said. 'It's not because of David at all. This year I decided to celebrate in my own home. You know, this will be my third Christmas in this house and I've always been away.'

'But Brendan and I miss you, darling.' Sara tucked the dish-towel into its holder, lifting her shoulders on a deep sigh. 'And we were worried about you being on your own. We were so looking forward to sharing Christmas with you and David.'

Holly was making a tray of coffee and she looked up sharply. 'Mother, I know you liked David, but there was nothing between us in a romantic sense.'

'I blame Martin,' her mother murmured impatiently. 'I know you didn't tell us the whole story of your broken engagement, just as I know he's prevented you from finding happiness with another man.'

'Nonsense!' Holly tried to sound indignant. 'Martin was a long time ago and he certainly has nothing to do with me choosing to celebrate Christmas at home this year.'

'And has Dr Caine?' Sara Lewis asked curiously.

'He's a good friend,' Holly admitted, shocked that her mother was so perceptive.

'Another one!' Sara snorted.

Holly picked up the tray and tried to ignore the colour which surged into her cheeks. 'He told you at supper, Mother, he's going back to the States at Easter. Now stop trying to play Cupid. Come along and let's have our coffee.'

Holly's vision of her day tomorrow, spent alone with Reece, was slowly diminishing. She had already accepted that tonight they would have to part, instead of cuddling up in her bed and waking to a lazy breakfast and a whole day ahead of them. Now she was beginning to think, well-founded though her mother's intentions were, they were about to ruin her Christmas.

'Who's running the hotel while you're away?' In the sitting room Holly poured coffee, reluctant to meet Reece's gaze which she felt boring into her back.

'Your mother decided she wanted some redecoration done so we've closed,' Brendan said in his mild-mannered way. There was no doubt, Holly reflected, who was boss in her family. Brendan might be a couple of years younger than her mother, but it was Sara who ruled the roost. 'But at least we've been able to come here,' he added cheerfully.

At that moment Holly turned to pass Reece his coffee and was dismayed to see the disappointment in his eyes as she raised her eyebrows in silent apology. They hadn't even been able to snatch a few minutes together, and all through supper her mother had fired questions at him. Now, it seemed, with no hotel to return to, her parents were planning on staying indefinitely.

'You shouldn't have driven all this way just for me,' Holly remarked, trying to compose herself.

'Not at all,' Sara said. 'As Brendan says, the change of scenery is wonderful. And, to save putting you to any trouble, we'll take you out to lunch on Christmas Day, perhaps at that nice hotel near the harbour.'

'But—' Holly began, only to be stopped in mid-sentence as her mother continued, without taking a breath. Sara turned her attention to Reece, her grey eyes going curiously over the handsome doctor who sat with his long legs outstretched in her daughter's front room.

Holly felt the last of her hope slip away. Unknown to her well-intended mother, she was to be robbed of her one day with Reece over the Christmas holiday and there was simply nothing at all she could do about it.

It was not until the Sunday after Christmas that Holly's tiny house became her own again. After breakfast Brendan drove the BMW from its parking spot outside and Sara waved her daughter goodbye, managing to elicit assurances of a visit to Cumbria in the early spring.

Afterwards Holly sat on the bar stool in the kitchen and poured herself a fresh coffee. Almost six days had passed since she had seen Reece. He had phoned her, though their conversation had been minimal because of her house-guests. Having taken the week off from work, there had been no chance of talking to him at the practice. She could hardly wait to see him again and she wondered if she dared telephone Chartwell to explain she was on her own once more.

With difficulty she decided to restrain her impetuosity. It was a kind of unwritten rule she adhered to—never to bother the doctors at home—and, besides, asking for Reece if Peter or Marge answered would arouse suspicion.

Several times during her parents' stay she had asked herself why she was bothering with the secrecy. Had she not been concerned that the truth would cause embarrassment to them, for they would then realise the awkwardness of their unannounced visit, she would have been tempted to reveal the affair.

However, since Reece had been on call over the holiday and had not suggested a meeting, she had decided to avoid any major revelations. As she sat quietly, sipping her coffee, she was glad she'd kept silent. Her mother and step-father would probably never meet Reece again so what would have been the point?

Holly tidied the house and washed the sheets from the guest-room bed which her parents had occupied. She removed the little Christmas tree whose branches were now brown and barren, changed into the soft blue Angora sweater her mother had bought her and drew her hair up into a shining chignon. Every moment she expected the telephone to ring and when it did at four o'clock she ran to it, her heart beating wildly.

She was disappointed to hear the voice of Judith Stone, the new practice manager, who was to start at the surgery the following day. Trying to inject a note of enthusiasm into her own voice, Holly exchanged pleasantries and listened as Judith apologised for phoning. She wondered when Holly was due to begin work again so that she had some idea of the schedules, before arriving on Monday morning.

After answering Judith's questions, she rang off and stared at the silent instrument. Why hadn't Reece telephoned? she wondered. The prospect of not seeing him until tomorrow at work depressed her. Doubts began to fill her mind as she allowed herself to speculate on why he hadn't visited, even on a friendly pretext, whilst her mother and Brendan had been present.

She told herself he had probably arrived at the same conclusion she had, deciding it would be unwise to try to explain their agreed arrangement of a temporary relationship, and so had concluded that the sensible thing to do was to avoid any further contact while her family remained.

But when the telephone remained silent for the rest of the evening her fears steadily deepened, fears that convinced her he had come to another decision during their enforced separation— that the affair was better ended here rather than at Easter. Almost certainly when he saw her again she would have to prepare herself to accept this decision.

On Monday Holly found herself early at the surgery, despite her attempts to pace herself while showering and dressing. To boost her spirits she had put on a newly purchased uniform and washed her hair and bobbed it, its longer, heavy length complementing her regular features. She could do nothing, she realised, about the apprehension in her large grey eyes, but she hoped that when she walked into the surgery she would be able to face the scrutiny of the girls at Reception, without giving anything away.

As it was, she need not have worried because it was the day before New Year's Eve and there were several patients in a celebratory mood, bringing in gifts for the New Year. Boxes of chocolates, biscuits and sweets were displayed in Reception from grateful patients and Jo and Kathy were in high spirits, talking of the approach of New Year.

Holly joined in briefly, then left for the office, a tingle of apprehension going down her spine as she passed Reece's door. It was closed and, although surgery had not yet begun, she assumed he was busy.

Turning into the office, she found Peter and Reece in conversation. Both of them looked around at her as she entered.

'Holly!' Peter called cheerfully. 'Surfacing from Christmas, are you?'

She managed to smile brightly, catching Reece's gaze. 'Just about, thanks, Peter. What about you?'

'Best Christmas in years,' Peter said, beaming at her. 'All due to this man, of course. Covered the whole of the festive season for us.'

Reece did not take his eyes from her face and sudden hope flickered as she tried to read his expression.

'Did you drive up north to your parents?' Peter asked as he frowned in an effort to recall her plans.

'No, this year they came to me,' she said. Deliberately looking at Reece, she added, 'They returned to Cumbria yesterday morning.'

Peter made several more comments, then gathered his stick, which he had propped against the desk, and was about to leave when Judith opened the door and stopped short. She was a small, fair woman in her mid-forties and behind the owlish spectacles a pair of intelligent brown eyes widened as she gazed at the three of them. 'Oh, sorry,' she apologised, clutching an armful of records to her chest. 'It was you I was looking for, Dr Peter, regarding one or two queries.'

'Come in, Judith,' said Reece briskly. 'Which reminds me, I've one or two queries myself, Holly, which I need to draw your attention to. Come into my room, will you, please?'

Holly felt the colour fly into her cheeks at the barked command as both Judith and Peter looked in her direction. Awkwardly she nodded and turned to walk out, aware of the silence in the room as she left.

Moments later in the hall Reece was about to speak when Bronwyn appeared, showing a patient into his consulting room. 'Mrs Bradbury, Dr Caine,' she called, and Reece nodded, his tall form standing uncertainly in the middle of the passageway.

The moment the coast was clear he moved towards Holly. 'Are you really alone in the house?' he asked in a tight voice.

'Yes,' she said, startled. 'As I said to Peter, they left yesterday.'

'I've promised to accompany Marge and Peter to some dinner organised by one of the drug companies. Will you be in at six?'

She nodded, her heart sinking as she realised it was to be only a brief visit. Before he could say more, another patient appeared at the top of the corridor and they started to walk in opposite directions, Reece to his consulting room and she back into Reception, where she searched for the nurse's book in a distracted fashion. Why had he been so cool, so distant? Had it anything to do with what he wanted to say to her tonight? Unable to find the book she was searching for and realising it must be back in the office, she retraced her steps, reluctant to come face to face with Peter and Judith again.

She felt yet more embarrassment as Peter, who was now seated at the desk, and Judith, in a chair beside him, looked up. Holly picked up the book which lay on the shelf and, murmuring an apology, hurried from the room.

Continuing to be beset by doubts over her meeting with Reece and apprehensive of the one to come, Holly found her day growing progressively worse. All her patients seemed to have complaints. One elderly patient expostulated at length over the neglect she'd felt from her family during Christmas. Another woman with severe arthritis insisted she had been besieged by demanding relatives who had caused her painful complaint to flare up. Jonathan was in a trough of despondency at not receiving a Christmas card from Gary Sharpe, and when she drove past Ben's little cottage her heart tightened at the sight of the unlit windows.

By five, reluctant to return home, she drove slowly, trying to blank her mind to what might lay ahead, but when she turned into her street the Volvo was already parked outside her house.

Instead of taking her into his arms, Reece walked ahead into the front room and stood for a few seconds at the window, before turning slowly to look at her. 'Am I to take it,' he said quietly, 'you've had second thoughts regarding us?'

She was astonished and, without removing her coat, walked towards him. 'Whatever do you mean?'

'I would have thought it was obvious. You made it plain you'd rather I didn't call while your family was here. And after what Brendan told me about your ex-fiancé—'

'Martin?' she floundered. 'What did Brendan say about Martin?'

'He said how upset your mother was when you'd decided

to cry off the wedding at the last moment. I've been mulling it over in my mind and, as you avoided any contact with me over Christmas, I assumed you'd had a similar change of heart with me.'

'That's unfair,' she gasped in dismay. 'It's a fact my mother was very upset when I cancelled all the arrangements and I know Brendan was concerned for her, but neither of them have any real understanding of the events which led up to the cancelling of the wedding. And, most importantly, my decision two years ago bears no relationship at all to how I feel about you.'

Reece frowned, his voice low. 'But it's true that you decided to back out of the wedding?'

'Yes, it's true,' Holly admitted defensively, 'but there were reasons for that which I've never discussed with anyone, least of all Brendan or my mother. And if you draw any parallels between Cassandra and me you're very much mistaken.' The words had flown from her mouth before she'd thought, and the expression that came over Reece's face was one of shock.

'Cassandra...' he muttered. 'Who told you about Cassandra?'

Holly hesitated but now she had no option but to explain. 'That day at Chartwell, when I accompanied Peter back, he explained briefly that Cassandra had left you on the day of your wedding. I can assure you, Reece, whatever her reasons were for doing such a cruel thing to you they could in no way mirror the reasons I decided to end my engagement to Martin.'

He stared at her slightly tilted chin and flushed cheeks and the deep frown on his brow slowly cleared as what she said slowly seemed to make an impression on him. After a few moments of silence he said quietly, 'So I'm wrong? You do still want to see me?'

'How could you think otherwise?' she asked quietly. He

moved towards her and pulled her into his arms, instantly easing the deep sense of loss which had pervaded her since Sunday morning. 'Oh, Reece, what's happened to us?' she whispered, laying her face on his warm chest as his strong arms hugged her. 'Why are we so insecure about each other?'

'Brendan started me thinking, I suppose,' he said. 'I wondered if you were relieved to have the company over Christmas in order to cool our relationship.'

'Then we both drew the wrong conclusions,' she sighed, looking up. 'I have to admit to wondering if you had decided much the same. I know we agreed we would keep seeing each other until Easter but I also recognised there was a chance you might change your mind.' Her voice was shaky. 'You know, I wanted to tell you about Martin the night we visited Josie and stopped at the True Lovers' Knot. I see now I should have.'

'Oh, Holly,' he sighed, holding her head between his hands, 'quite frankly nothing matters now—only that we don't waste any more time.' He drew her against his chest once more, holding her quietly so that all she could hear was the steady pounding of his heart under her ear. Relief and anxiety went through her in twin bursts as she thought again how fraught a transient affair such as theirs could become.

'How long can you stay?' she asked.

He gave a short, mirthless laugh. 'There's no way I can avoid being dragged out to this blessed dinner.'

She nodded, wearily accepting that once again important issues were to be shelved. 'When shall I see you next?'

'Tomorrow,' he suggested at once. 'Marge is on call. I'll have the whole evening free and the next day until five when I take over from her.''

She gazed up at him, crooking her eyebrow. 'Tomorrow is New Year's Eve. Don't you want to celebrate?'

He nodded slowly. 'Oh, yes, I've every intention of celebrating, my darling, so you'd better get in some beauty sleep because tomorrow night you won't be getting a wink.' And this time he bent to kiss her.

New Year's Eve, Holly decided, very nearly made up for the travesty of Christmas.

Reece brought champagne and, locking the door, they took the bottle and glasses to the bedroom where, thirsty only for the taste of one another, they made love immediately.

Yet again no words were spoken, no explanations given, as they spent the hours before twelve making love with an urgency that both knew came from the insecurity of the past days. Just before midnight Reece remembered to uncork the champagne and filled their glasses on the last stroke of twelve. Amidst the champagne-damp sheets they toasted the arrival of New Year, finally laying aside their half-full glasses to sample the sweet provocativeness of each other's lips. This time they made love with a slow, searching delight which filled the early morning hours until at last they fell asleep, curled up together, while a half-moon gleamed in through the window from the dawn sky, making way for the passage of another orb which would first grow crimson and then gold to announce the first day of a brand new year.

The following Monday Ken Filler sat with Reece and Holly in his office, a small room he had converted at the back of his house. His brow was deeply furrowed. 'I'm scared,' he admitted, 'that life is going to slip away from my control. Gone are pub lunches with my colleagues or trips to the theatre with my wife because getting there just isn't easy any more. Up till now the worst episodes have cleared up.

The steroid injections help, but what if they don't one day? Perhaps one day I won't be able to get out of bed.'

After a painstaking thirty-minute physical examination of his patient Reece packed away his case. 'Approximately seventy per cent of sufferers are still able to be actively engaged in normal pursuits five years after diagnosis,' he told Ken reflectively. 'And I see no reason why you shouldn't carry on in the way you are.'

'It isn't as easy as all that. Because of the MS you find your social circle narrows and your friends drop away,' protested Ken.

'Let's look at what you have achieved and what you can do,' Reece suggested. 'You're fortunate in your work being home-based—you've managed to keep your clients and you've a wonderful garden, which you maintain very well.'

'Not without effort,' Ken sighed. 'I feel so weak and lifeless I haven't really the heart to go out there sometimes.'

'The weakness in your legs and the problem with your co-ordination can be improved with physio.'

Ken shrugged and then, as he shifted uncomfortably in his seat, he looked up at Reece. 'All the physio in the world isn't going to help being stuck at home. We feel so isolated.'

Reece was silent for a moment then took out his notes and after a few seconds began to write. 'Phone this number. This is a society set up for sufferers of MS. Don't be afraid to get in touch with them. They will be able to help you with counselling and they provide a news-sheet which will connect you to other people offering help and support.'

While they were there, Holly dressed a small burn Ken had sustained on his arm from the gas cooker. Every so often he 'was in the wars', as his wife put it, and Holly was swift to check for new bumps and bruises. This time the red but not infected penny-sized burn was beginning to harden and therefore needed only swift attention with a mild antiseptic.

The next call which they had decided to make was to Martha Macreedy. When they arrived, the warden was trying to persuade a recalcitrant Martha to get out of bed. Calmly Reece sat beside her and picked up her hand, giving her a lopsided smile guaranteed to melt anyone's heart.

Martha was fairly lucid, despite the previous hour which the warden had weathered with some fortitude. 'The trouble is I don't know how long I can go on spending so much time with her each day,' the warden sighed. 'I do my best, but I've twenty-four other residents to check on. She won't go into a rest home. Says it would be like going to prison.'

Holly brought her attention back to Reece who finally rose to his feet. Martha looked at Holly sulkily and pulled up the sheet. The room had an unpleasant odour and all the contents were disorderly, her dressing-table piled high with junk.

When they left her, Reece called at the warden's flat and delivered a prescription for an antibiotic. 'The glucose starvation is causing her extreme exhaustion,' he explained, 'and she's developed a rather nasty boil on her neck. This should help to clear up the infection.'

'It isn't going to help her head much, though,' the warden observed, but took the prescription all the same. 'She really needs to be in care.'

The comment was grounded in some truth, Holly reflected as she followed Reece to the cars.

'I wonder…' Reece sighed as he glanced back to the flats. 'I've a patient who runs a good nursing home in Conway Road. Perhaps I'll have a word.' Looking down at her, he added in a quiet voice, 'I heard this morning that Ben's cremation is scheduled for Thursday.'

Ben Sharman's cremation took place in Durnweston and the small service afterwards was given in the country chapel just outside Cancreel. Both Reece and Holly went to the simple service, attended by his neighbours, his home-care worker and a stranger who sat in the back pew.

It was a day of bright sun and crisp, clear skies, a hopeful reminder of spring, as they filed out into the chapel's court-yard. The man in the dark suit who had occupied the back pew approached them.

'Dr Caine, Miss Edmunds?' he asked, and when they nodded he drew them to one side.

'I represent Pullman and Fryer, the late Mr Sharman's solicitors,' he began to explain. 'You will be receiving a letter from us but Mr Fryer suggested, should I see you, that I notify you that we've invited you, Dr Caine and Miss Edmunds, to attend a brief meeting with us next week.'

Reece look surprised. 'In connection with Mr Sharman?'

The tall, dour-looking man nodded. 'Our client has left a final request which Mr Fryer would like to discuss with you. Perhaps if you telephone our office we could arrange a mutually convenient time?'

Reece agreed, though he was still frowning as the man thanked him and turned away to hurry down the church path. Reece glanced at Holly with raised eyebrows. 'Now, what do you think that was all about?'

'He said a request of some sort.' Holly shrugged.

'Whatever it is,' Reece sighed, 'I wish we had known of it before Ben died rather than now when nothing we can do will make any real difference one way or the other.'

It was a remark Reece was to remember when, after morning surgery on the following Wednesday, they arrived at the offices of Pullman and Fryer for the scheduled meet-ing.

'There are two outstanding matters,' explained Mr Fryer, as soon as they had taken their seats in the tiny office. 'The late Mr Sharman added a codicil to his will. There was a small sum of money kept aside in a post office account. He instructed that it be given to your practice, Dr Caine, and donated to any needy patient deserving of financial help, in appreciation for your kindness towards him.'

'But I treated him only for the last three months of his life,' Reece answered in surprise. 'Miss Edmunds knew him for far longer than I did.'

'In his instructions to us he remarked on the care both you and Miss Edmunds gave him and wanted you to know you supported him through a very difficult time.' Mr Fryer smiled hesitantly. 'And there was one more favour he asked. Mr Sharman wished for his ashes to be scattered at sea, and he further asked that you and Miss Edmunds specifically carry out this duty.'

CHAPTER TEN

REECE raked a hand through his black hair, his deep blue eyes roaming intently over the faces at the January practice meeting. Doctors and staff had just voted on the subject of the cheque which lay on the desk in the corner of the staff-room. 'So, we're all agreed that from the donation Ben Sharman left us a computer will be purchased for Jonathan Avis?'

Everyone nodded and there were soft murmurings of agreement as Reece hesitated for the last time, before scribbling on the pad before him. How wonderful it was, Holly thought with a pang of deep satisfaction, when something like this happened. If only Ben were here he would have been delighted, she thought sadly, and then gave a wistful smile to herself as she realised that if Ben had still been alive this opportunity for Jonathan would never have arisen.

'Last on the agenda is Martha Macreedy,' said Reece, and the murmurings stopped. 'I think we are all abreast of her condition. The problem is what to do about it. We could try for daily nursing, involving the district and community nurses, or there is a place available at Greenhills in Conway Road. I've made tentative enquiries and I think Martha would eventually fit into Don and Gill Miller's nursing home. However, it's a question of balancing her state of mind and the safety factor with the trauma of removing her from her home. Has anyone any suggestions?'

Peter shifted in his chair. 'Martha's lived in Cancreel all her life. She grew up and lived in her parents' house, caring for them until they died. Then she went straight into sheltered accommodation where she remains to this day.'

'So, basically, you think we should try to manage her where she is?'

'For the time being, yes,' Peter answered firmly.

Reece nodded and with a fleeting glance at Holly bent to write once more. When the meeting was over Holly mingled with the others, enjoying a cup of tea before leaving. It was a cold, bright evening and the sky revealed a breathtaking sunset and dark blue clouds, a sure sign of another good day tomorrow.

Reece caught her up, his jacket buttoned to his chin against the brisk wind. 'I'm on call so I can't stop,' he told her, glancing across to the surgery where everyone was trailing out. 'I'm concerned over our decision with Martha, but I don't want to undermine Peter's suggestion of leaving her for the time being.'

Holly nodded, pulling the collar of her coat to her ears. 'I'm worried, too.' She glanced once more at Bronwyn and Jo who were, despite their attempts to disguise it, curiously staring in their direction.

Reece grinned. 'I'd better let you go. We're causing congestion on the pavement.'

Holly felt her cheeks go pink. 'Can you make Friday? I thought about cooking something special.'

'Done.' He chuckled under his breath and leaned forward, stopping fractionally short of kissing her. 'One day I'm going to forget,' he growled, and moved back. 'I'll ring you later.'

As he moved away, Holly avoided glancing across the road and made a bolt around her car. Unlocking it and bundling her things inside, she sank into the seat with a sigh. As she started the car she happened to catch Bronwyn's gaze. Although they were separated by the width of the road Holly saw her expression, a mixture of curiosity and recognition, as she half turned, not quite making up her mind to walk away as Reece crossed back to where his car was parked.

Holly drove down the hill to the harbour where she parked the car for ten minutes and waited to allow Reece time to say goodnight, jump in the Volvo and drive away, though she wondered why she was bothering with all the secrecy when her feelings for Reece outweighed any concern she might have had for the opinion of others.

A small voice pierced the low hum of early morning patients and, despite the long Monday morning queues, Holly was impaled against the wall by a large white bear as Josie Dobson fell into her arms. 'I'm feeling much better now and Bear is too.' Josie gave her another huge hug. 'But we still have to go back to hospital for tests.' Holly returned the hug, aware Reece had emerged from the consulting room with Mary. 'Mummy brought us for a check-up because Bear had a sore ear too,' went on Josie brightly. 'She said it will save you coming to the house for once now we're out of hospital.'

Mary had said goodbye to Reece and was walking towards them. 'We've brought in some chocolates to say thank you,' she called brightly, 'because we missed you at Christmas. Josh and Josie seemed to think you two might like to eat them together.' Josie's mum lifted an eyebrow, inviting comment, but fortunately Bronwyn beckoned from the desk and it was too late for Holly to say anything other than a brief word of thanks.

'Dr Caine would like to see you before you leave, Holly,' Bronwyn told her as the receptionist gave her a long and thoughtful stare.

'Is he free now?' Holly tried to sound casual.

Bronwyn nodded, but Holly felt her curious stare on her back as she made her way to his consulting room. She knocked, deliberately loudly, and awaited the summons from inside. However, Reece's warm smile dispelled all her anxiety as she closed the door behind her, remembering as she looked at him the wonderful evening they had enjoyed together on Friday when she had cooked an exotic supper—concocting dishes they'd never tried before and enjoying every minute as they'd shared endless laughter over their laboured attempts with chopsticks.

It was not the memory of the cuisine that now brought colour to her cheeks under the two wings of chestnut hair which fell across her face, but the memory of later when, after the savoured and exquisite hours of love-making, they had fallen asleep, her body curved into his, until the intrusion of the alarm at eight the next morning.

Her one regret was that they had not spoken on a deeper level, as she had planned. The night had been so full of sparkle she had abandoned thoughts of referring to subjects which might have threatened their mood. When he had left her at nine to take a Saturday morning surgery she had rolled into the warm space he had left and laid her face on the indent of the pillow, her mind and body too saturated with pleasure to have any lasting pangs of regret.

Now, too, her heart gave a leap as he stared at her, the deep blue eyes regarding her across the room, eyes which had looked up from the pillow on Saturday morning, dreamy and lazy, recalling for her in their expression the intimate excitement of their lovemaking.

'You look wonderful,' he said quietly, 'and all I wanted was to see you. That's all.'

She was afraid to move closer because she couldn't trust herself not to rush into his arms. Instead she smiled, content to devour him with her eyes. 'And I wanted to see you. But I couldn't think of any excuse.'

He looked amused. 'It seems we don't need any these days. I'm sure your detours into my room have only caused eyebrows to raise moderately. No one has actually caught us red-handed, though I have to admit it's been close.' For a moment their eyes met, then he said, 'Did Mary tell you that since our visit to the hospital Josie's taken it into her head we're an item?'

Holly shrugged, smiling. 'Well, we were holding hands that night.'

'And kids are perceptive.'

'So...is that why you held my hand? Did you want Josie to know?'

He paused. 'I suppose, subconsciously, yes, I think I want everyone to know. But I don't want to make life difficult for you either now or later—and this is a small community.' He shrugged. 'I just manage by the skin of my teeth to remember that I won't be here for very much longer.'

'I'm trying hard not to think about it,' Holly responded quietly. 'It is, after all, what we agreed, isn't it?'

Sounds from outside suddenly made Holly jump. Taking a deep breath, she opened the door to the hubbub outside. 'Oh, heavens, it's bedlam,' she sighed.

Reece rolled his eyes and grinned. 'No peace for the not-so-wicked,' he said and Holly laughed.

'I'm not so sure about that.'

He quirked an eyebrow. 'So you're beginning to see through my façade?'

'And enjoying every moment,' she teased. 'I'll tell Bronwyn you're free.'

Vera Filler met Holly on her Wednesday visit with the news that her husband had begun physio again and had been driven to hospital by a volunteer from the MS society.

'This couple, Bill Forbes and his wife, Ann,' she went on to explain, 'are theatre lovers, too. He and his wife took us with them to Durnweston to see *Scrooge*, put on by the amateur dramatics club. It was so nice to get out and about again. As a matter of fact, the production was so good we bought two tickets for their new one at Easter.'

The mention of Easter, Holly realised, had a depressing effect on her, though she was happy for Vera's and Ken's new interest in life. However, for her Easter signalled the point of Reece's departure when she would have to resume her existence as it had been before he'd come into her life. Although spring had always been her favourite season, now the prospect of warm, lighter evenings filled with the scent of apple blossom and cut grass sent a pain across her heart because Reese wouldn't be there to experience it with her.

Suddenly the price she had been willing to pay when she had agreed to her temporary relationship with Reece now seemed impossibly high for she had never expected her emotions to run as deeply as this. She reflected honestly, however, that she wasn't fool enough to think that if she were given the chance again her choices would be any different to those she'd made last year.

With this in mind, she made her way to Jonathan's. As always, Gwen opened the door but there was something different in the atmosphere and Holly sensed it immediately as Gwen led the way to the lounge.

'I can't believe the news,' Jonathan told her, his face showing the old signs of animation. 'Dr Peter came last week to tell me about the computer but I still can't believe it.'

Holly had been so preoccupied she'd entirely forgotten the outcome of the practice meeting. She took a seat beside the wheelchair. In answer to Jonathan's questions regarding the donor, she told him how much Ben would have wanted the money to be of use to someone who deserved it as much as Jonathan. She repeated the details once more as Gwen and Doug came into the room and, although they were already aware of what had happened, they were eager for any small details which Holly could supply.

Peter had already spent time with Jonathan in order to ascertain what his requirements would be for hardware and software, choices which, apparently, had caused many hours of excitement since.

'We should never have been able to afford a computer,' Gwen said as she gazed at Holly. 'It's such perfect timing for Jonathan.'

Her son nodded. 'I've accepted I'm never going to walk,' he admitted quietly. 'I know I have to come to terms with my disability. It isn't the end of the world, not seeing Gary any more or thinking I shan't be able to ride—that was a selfish way of thinking.' He glanced at his parents. 'Mum and Dad need some time to themselves after all they've been through so I'm going to the day centre now. With that and the computer, I know I've a good chance of making a new life for myself.'

Gwen sniffed and Doug slipped an arm around her shoulder. 'We are so grateful for what the surgery has done,' Doug said in a low tone.

And for what you have done for us, Holly thought as she recalled the conversation she had had with Peter after he had come back from breaking the news of the computer to Jonathan. He had explained he had found a fresh sense of fulfilment through his chats with Jonathan, and though he had begun to feel frustrated and redundant after his stroke he had realised he could now relate to physical disability and help patients in a way he had never been able to before. From her own point of view, she had watched Reece's determination to encourage Jonathan to face his disability, an important lesson which she would have failed to learn otherwise.

And then there was Ben. His death had not been in vain, a thought expressed by Gwen as she frowned at Holly. 'We'd like to show our appreciation to the man who left the money for the computer,' she remarked, 'but I suppose we are too late. His funeral's over isn't it?'

Holly nodded, but another thought occurred to her. 'By Ben's own request his ashes will be scattered at sea,' she told them. 'You could have a floral tribute made up to put in the water. I'm sure it would be appropriate.'

Gwen was delighted. 'Do you know when it's happening?'

Holly knew that Reece had begun arrangements to hire a boat on which the memorial service would take place. 'Hopefully, at the end of February or the beginning of March,' she said.

'Oh, that gives us plenty of time,' Gwen said in a relieved voice. 'It just wouldn't have seemed right to accept such a lovely gift, without saying some kind of thank you.'

The visit had lifted her spirits, Holly realised as she travelled back to the surgery. She was happy to discover that a similar sense of well-being enveloped the waiting room as she entered, though there were no patients. Three cheerful faces stood outside Peter's room as Tim and Peter talked with Judith.

'Oh, Holly!' Peter exclaimed jubilantly, 'you're just in time to hear the good news. We think we've found a new partner, at least Tim has—someone he knew from university who had been working abroad and now wants to settle in this country. Her name is Celia Morton.'

'That's good news,' Holly said, unable to prevent her stomach from lurching. 'When will we have a chance of meeting her?'

'Nothing is definite yet,' cautioned Tim, 'but the interview will be during the second week in February,'

'I've set aside the fourteenth,' Judith added, glancing at her notes, 'and I'm organising a buffet from an outside caterers for lunchtime. So make a note in your diary, Holly.'

Holly didn't need to. She knew every day by heart until Easter. 'Yes. I will, Judith,' she said politely. 'Does Reece know?' The question was out before she had time to think, and all four faces turned to stare at her. Peter quickly broke the silence by shaking his head and grinning. 'No, but he soon will. Here he comes now.'

February brought with it a cold and marbled sky and a watery sun which shone behind tiny, scudding clouds. Peter's news had shocked Holly. With Celia Morton arriving for an interview, it could only mean that Reece's departure was certain. To all intents and purposes, she reflected, it had never been thought of as otherwise. She realised she had unwisely allowed herself to retain a vain, secret hope that his leaving might be postponed in the event of a replacement partner or locum not being found, a hope which she now saw disappearing in the form of Celia Morton.

It was Sunday and the smell of the roasting capon she was cooking filtered through from the kitchen. Reece had intended to have lunch with her, but he had telephoned to say he was still at Chartwell and Tim, who was due to take the on-call duty, had not yet contacted him.

Guessing it would probably be some time before he arrived, Holly gazed at the dusty corners of the house and considered the jobs she could attempt while she waited, but none of them appealed. She felt restless and preoccupied and, after wandering aimlessly around the house, finally decided that what she'd like most was a long, brisk walk over the cliffs and down to the sea where the change of scenery might distract her from the debilitating feeling of emptiness.

Changing into walking boots, warm black leggings and a fleece-lined anorak, she turned off the oven and set the chicken to cool on the top. Winter air sliced against her cheeks as she closed her front door and walked the steady gradient to the lane which led to the small car park at the base of the cliffs.

She crossed it and took the steps briskly, breathing in the air she so badly needed. When she reached the summit she strode along the cliff-top, her long legs taking her to a windy crest where she stood and stared out over the glittering blue ocean.

The water sparkled, little dots of sunlight catching the waves as they rolled in to crash against the rocks below. She gazed for long moments at the breathtaking sight, adjusting her eyes to the brightness of blue sea, emerald green grass and white-topped surf, before she suddenly noticed the thin plume of grey on the horizon.

Before she could decide what it was, a voice made her turn sharply, her heart picking up speed as a figure hurried towards her, instantly familiar despite the heavy walking boots and navy blue reefer.

'How's that for telepathy?' Reece panted as he jogged towards her, breathing hard from his sprint up the slope. His presence at once gave meaning to her day as he took her into his arms.

'How did you find me?' Holly's heart beat wildly as she drew her fingers over his broad shoulders.

'Guessed you might have gone for a walk. I couldn't imagine you not wanting to make the most of an afternoon like this, and when Tim arrived just as I put the phone down, after speaking to you, I decided I would change into this gear just in case. I was tempted to phone you back but I thought I'd give you a surprise. The Volvo's in the car park and we can collect it on our way home.'

She hadn't realised until she'd seen his figure rushing towards her how much she'd missed him, and it was a few moments before she could wrench her gaze from the strong, chiselled jaw and deep blue eyes, which were almost identical in colour to the swirling sea beneath them. She finally remembered the thin trail of grey on the horizon.

'You've arrived in time to help me make up my mind. What do you think that is out there?' She raised her hand to shield her eyes and they both gazed out to sea.

'It's smoke,' Reece decided after a few moments and, taking her hand, drew her with him to the cliff fence. They concentrated, narrowing their eyes, as the wind whistled around their ears. 'Hard to say exactly what it might be,' Reece muttered, 'but it's big—a tanker of some kind, perhaps. I think we'd better find out if the coastguard has been alerted. It will be quickest to ring from the car-phone.'

Retracing their steps, they hurried to the car park where Reece unlocked the Volvo and dialled the coastguard. Holly saw from his face that it was bad news.

'Fire aboard ship,' he mouthed, and after some discussion he replaced the mobile in the console. 'I'm afraid I was right. She's a foreign tanker, carrying crude palm oil—not toxic, thank God, but it could make a mess if there was a spill into the sea.'

'Is that likely?'

Reece shook his head. 'Not so far. They've contained the fire in the engine room, but the master has asked for medical assistance. They're sending out a civilian helicopter equipped with medical supplies which acts in co-ordination with the coastguard. I've told them I'll go out with it if the pilot can land on the cliff. It's a natural platform for a chopper.' He looked down at her and reached to tug up the collar of her anorak, his fingers gently tucking in the wild strands of her wind-blown hair. 'I'm sorry about our afternoon.'

She gazed at him levelly. 'If there's room I'd like to come, too.'

'I don't think so, my sweet. It could be dangerous.'

'But I might be some help and at least I won't be staring

uselessly at the ship from the top of a cliff, wondering if you'll be all right.'

He laughed softly, held her face between his hands and gazed at her. 'How do you feel about flying in one of those things?'

She smiled. 'As long as I'm with you...'

He studied her for a few seconds more, then he locked the Volvo, turned to take her hand and they scrambled up the steps once more until finally they reached the cliff-top again.

On the plateau they waited for the helicopter. Although Holly had never flown in one before, she had never had qualms about air travel. If she experienced a twinge of apprehension now it soon passed as Reece gripped her hand tightly while they waited on the wind-swept summit.

Faintly at first came the low throbbing sound of the approaching aircraft, a tiny black dot in the air, no larger than a seagull. Then surprisingly swiftly it circled over them, descending in an ear splitting whine of rotors.

'Keep your head down and hang on to me,' Reece shouted. Holly ducked, running beside him as the grass flattened out like a carpet around them. Hauled inside by a member of the crew, Holly found herself safely in the belly of the great machine, which was far larger than it had looked in the air. Once in their seats, she managed to gulp back her breath as the pilot took them sharply upwards in a stomach-turning ascent.

Reece leaned across and put his mouth close to her ear. 'Are you all right?' She nodded, swallowing, and he squeezed her hand.

The next moment they were soaring high above the ground. Reece gave her one more reassuring glance before he rose to his feet and made his way towards the pilot.

Holly braced herself to look out of the small window, but was surprised to find the aerial view was so magnificent it overcame all her alarm. The green cliffs melted into blue, transparent sea until the water slowly darkened as the helicopter flew out into the deeper waters of the Atlantic.

Predictably her stomach dropped as they arced in the sky and a few seconds later she saw the dark plume of smoke and the ship beneath as the helicopter closed in.

'We're told there's only one casualty needing hospital attention,' Reece explained when he returned. 'If the smoke isn't too thick we're going to winch him up, but we're not sure exactly what's wrong. None of the crew speak good English.' His expression softened as he gave her arm another squeeze.

When he'd left her she cast her eyes over the medical equipment, relieved to see the blue and white cylinders of Entonox—a fifty-fifty mixture of oxygen and nitrous oxide which was useful to patients with limb fractures. All the other first-aid equipment was there, including pulse oximeter, defibrillator, nebuliser, peak-flow meters and airway, ventilation and circulation equipment.

It was at this point that she saw Reece disappear from the helicopter. Her heart beat faster as she turned to the window and watched as he was lowered to the vessel below. His body was attached to the recovery line and his helmeted head swaying precariously over the ocean below. A circle of men were gathered on the deck, their faces anxiously upturned as the line swung over them. Then she lost sight of him as the smoke, blown by a sudden gust of wind, covered the helicopter in a thick grey blanket.

There was a terrible acrid smell and the helicopter seemed briefly to lose height. In those moments she experienced a sense of imbalance which caused her to hold her breath anxiously until at last the wind changed and, with clear vision restored, she saw that Reece had landed safely.

While the casualty was being winched up, Holly busied herself with laying out the dressings they might need. It was a task she did slowly, almost mechanically, as the pounding of her heart and the noise in the interior of the helicopter seemed to increase.

It seemed an eternity before she dared to look, watching as both the patient and Reece were recovered and hoisted aboard. Again the acrid waft of smoke filled the air, but this time she hardly noticed as she gazed into Reece's smudged face. 'A bad ankle fracture, a head wound and minor burns,' he told her. 'Let's cut some of his damaged clothing cut away so we can see what we're doing.'

Despite groans from their patient, Holly managed to settle the young man on the small bed. His accent seemed to be Polish or Czech. She carefully removed the singed bits of clothing while Reece made a full examination of chest and limbs.

Together they worked quickly to administer first aid and painkiller, dressing the minor wounds as the man became less agitated. Finally immobilising the fractured ankle, Reece went up front and Holly heard him ask how long it would take to fly to Durnweston General.

'Fifteen minutes,' the pilot replied, and Reece nodded.

'That'll do. Now, get me back down, will you? I'll see how I can help the other casualties until the lifeboat manages to put a line across.'

Holly hadn't realised Reece was going aboard the vessel and for a few moments she was alarmed, but he smiled as he came towards her, bending to explain. 'There are minor casualties on board,' he told her, 'mainly smoke inhalation and a few burns which can be treated without having to remove the crew. The pilot will have you back in no time.'

The last she saw of him was his broad shoulders, shrugging on a medical pack and the intricate safety harness, but she preferred not to watch his departure again. Instead, she made her patient comfortable, checking pulse and respiration, and by the time she had done this the helicopter was circling the ship once more, ready to fly home, its mission accomplished.

The pilot was as good as his word and arrived at Durnweston in under a quarter of an hour. A and E doctors and nurses waited on the lawns of the hospital and, crumpled and grubby, Holly followed the little group, giving details of the young man's condition as they went.

Inside the hospital her legs finally stopped shaking. Finding herself a quiet corner in a comfortable chair, she let the wave of exhaustion wash over her now that she was able to relax. It was difficult to believe that only moments ago her feet had been on the floor of a helicopter.

The last time she'd been here had been with Reece when she'd waited anxiously for news of Neil Haigh. It seemed like yesterday and yet a lifetime ago. Now she was here again and so much had happened since that day at Chartwell when she had scrambled from the bath and discovered Reece on the other side of the door.

She smiled to herself at the memory, her eyelids heavy, as the helicopter flew noisily over the hospital roof.

Much later, Holly sat up on the chair where she had fallen asleep and blinked into a pair of tired blue eyes ringed with smudges of smoke, almost indistinguishable from the thick black hair strewn untidily across his forehead.

'You're back,' she breathed, as she blinked once more. 'How long have you been sitting there?'

He reached out for her hand, squeezed it tightly and grinned. 'Only a few minutes, that's all. The lifeguard ran me to the car park and I was able to collect the Volvo.'

As she smiled, the relief of seeing him back safe and sound was almost too much for her, and she bit down on her lip so that he would not see the tremble which threatened her mouth. 'How many casualties were there?' she asked, trying to regain her self-control.

'About half the crew were suffering from smoke inhalation and burns but nothing serious. They've managed to extinguish the fire and it's possible she'll be able to limp into port for repairs without the aid of tugs. There was some palm oil seepage, but nothing that can't be cleaned up safely without danger to the environment.'

She sank back in the chair, reluctant to move, content to have him beside her and know that he was safe. 'I suppose I'm overreacting,' she sighed, 'and this kind of rescue is all in a day's work for you, but I'm just so relieved you're back safely.'

His gaze went slowly over her face. Seeing the tiny tremble, which she had failed to disguise, he drew her closer. 'To be honest,' he said huskily, 'I'm not at all averse to a little overreaction now and then...'

For a long moment their eyes locked. She wasn't any good at hiding her feelings from him and now she wondered if he had guessed her secret. Did he have any idea at all that she was falling in love with him?

But if he had he didn't disclose it. 'I think it's time to go home,' he said. And, rising slowly from the chair, he drew her to her feet.

CHAPTER ELEVEN

CELIA Morton was a tall, attractive blonde and, like Tim, was in her early thirties. She had worked with a charity organisation in West Africa for the last year and had now decided to return to her roots in England. Originally from Somerset, she had heard from a mutual friend from university days of Tim's search to find a partner.

The interview had been scheduled for Friday in order that Celia could meet the majority of staff, and Judith had set aside an extra hour for lunch, organising a buffet in the staffroom so that the formalities were tempered by a degree of relaxed conversation.

Reece had offered to take any emergency calls and as Celia Morton was introduced to the girls at the desk, predictably, the telephone rang.

'It's the warden, Mrs Beale, calling about Martha Macreedy,' Bronwyn told Reece, who immediately separated himself from the three doctors, talking to Celia Morton. 'She thinks Martha's had an accident of some kind.'

'Tell her I'll be there in five minutes.' Reece glanced at Holly who, with Alison and Joy, had just finished speaking to Celia and raised his eyebrows.

She nodded at his unspoken summons and, gathering bag and coat, made her apologies and left with him for Martha's. When they arrived Mrs Beale allowed them entrance through the security door and led them to Martha's flat.

'I don't think she's broken anything and she's sitting up

163

all right,' Mrs Beale explained. 'But the flat is in a terrible state.'

'When did someone last check her?' Reece's tone was tactful enough but Mrs Beale looked upset.

'I can't keep looking in,' she complained. 'I buzz through every morning and at night, but at times she deliberately ignores me.'

'So you spoke to her this morning?'

'Yes. But she was confused so I called the community nurse and she came and only left about an hour ago.'

'Which means her diabetes has been checked,' murmured Reece with a frown. 'How did you find out she was in distress?'

The warden pushed open the door to the bathroom. 'She pulled that red cord there, which sets off an alarm.'

Martha lay on the bathroom floor, her back propped against the bath. She was still in her nightclothes. 'Hello, Martha, what happened?' Reece asked as he bent beside her.

'I got a different pain,' she muttered, 'but it's gone now. She made me sit here till you came.'

'What sort of pain?' Reece asked.

Martha said nothing, looking at them suspiciously. 'My feet got cramp and I tripped,' she eventually said.

'And you pulled the cord because of the foot pain?'

'Because of the cramp I couldn't get up.'

Reece nodded slowly. 'And there's nothing else you'd like to tell me?'

'I'd say if there was, wouldn't I?' Martha protested belligerently.

Holly knelt on Martha's other side and met Reece's glance. From behind them Mrs Beale made a sound of exasperation.

'We'll be fine now, Mrs Beale,' Reece said, looking up. 'Thank you for your help.'

Somewhat unwilling to leave, the warden finally departed and Martha grinned. 'She's an old fusspot. Thinks I can't look after myself. Wants to put me in a home.'

'So you didn't hurt yourself when you fell?' Holly tried to draw her back to the moment she had the accident.

'It was only her made me stay here,' Martha insisted. 'Look, I'll get up.' Before they could prevent her she tightened her lips and leaned forward, only to give a little gasp as she put her hand to her chest. Reece frowned and carefully settled her back against the bath again. He placed his stethoscope in the open V of her nightie and listened to her chest.

'How long have you had chest pain, Martha?' he asked as he took her blood pressure.

'You mean the indigestion,' said Martha stubbornly. 'It's from the horrible plastic food I get from those delivery people.'

Reece then examined her legs and, sliding off her slippers, carefully inspected her feet. Afterwards he replaced her slippers and, instructing Martha not to move, he drew Holly into the sitting room. 'BP's up and the cramp, I suspect, is due to the worsening artherosclerosis. Diabetics always run a higher risk of disease to the arteries and its attendant problems. She's fresh ulcers starting, too, though I can see the nurse has given them a good deal of attention. But what I am concerned with is the chest pain. It's angina we're looking at here, I'm sure. I'm going to admit her for an ECG and run her through some tests.'

'I don't think she'll agree easily,' Holly remarked.

'We'll give it a try,' murmured Reece. Returning to the bathroom, he began to talk to Martha.

To Holly's surprise, eventually Martha did agree, but not before Reece had exerted his fair share of gentle persuasion. While they waited for the ambulance Holly packed a case, managing to find a fresh nightdress and dressing-gown, a towel which had seen better days but was clean and the few toiletries Martha kept in her bathroom. The flat was in turmoil, though Mrs Beale said the home-care worker had called twice during the week. The most worrying thing of all was the four delivered lunches of the week, all uneaten and hidden in the cupboard under the stove.

At that point the meals-on-wheels lady arrived, bearing Friday's offering, and Holly explained what had happened. 'She never says a word.' The woman shrugged as she looked curiously around the flat. 'She'll won't let any of us in so we can never check on what she eats.'

Holly thanked the woman and was relieved to see the arrival of the ambulance. Mrs Beale emerged from her flat and gave the ambulance driver a carrier bag containing fruit, barley water and tissues.

'I'll visit soon,' said Mrs Beale as Martha was lifted on board.

'Don't trouble yourself,' muttered Martha rudely. 'And it's a hospital I'm going to, not a home.'

When the ambulance had gone they left Mrs Beale, tidying the flat. A bracing odour of disinfectant issued into the corridor behind them. Reece grinned. 'Mrs Beale is seizing her opportunity,' he remarked wryly as they left through the security doors.

'And despite Martha's antagonism I think she knows that without Mrs Beale's watchful eye she would never have coped,' Holly sighed as they sat in the Volvo.

'And therein lies the next problem.' Reece frowned. 'What to do with Martha. It's obvious now she'll have to go into care. We'll see what the hospital turns up and then look towards a few weeks' convalescence perhaps.'

Holly lifted her eyebrows. 'At Greenhills?'

Reece nodded. 'At Greenhills.'

They drove back to the practice where the buffet was in progress in the staffroom. As Holly and Reece walked in a few glances came their way, but Marge strode over. As Reece moved towards Celia, who was talking with Tim, Marge took Holly's arm and guided her to the laden work-top.

'Better than quiche,' said Marge. 'Our Judith is turning out to be a treasure. I can't think what we did without her.'

Holly agreed. She liked Judith a lot and even in the short time she had been at the surgery she had made impressive improvements in the schedules.

Choosing several wafer-thin sandwiches and some cheese and pineapple cubes on cocktail sticks, she hesitated before she asked her next question. 'Has Celia decided to take the partnership?' she finally managed to ask.

'We think so,' Marge answered in a quiet voice. 'She really would fit in well, I feel.'

It was an answer part of Holly had hoped not to hear. If Celia accepted it would mean Reece would be free to return to the States. But the other half of her knew how important it was for the practice to have a good doctor and Celia was a bonus insofar as female patients often preferred to consult a woman. As she thought of this she remembered Reece's words last year when she had first met him and he had remarked that Ben Sharman might prefer a male nurse.

At the time she had found it difficult to imagine a man of Ben's age worrying about his catheter change but Reece's point had been proved, as had his persistence with Jonathan and, today, his gentle persuasion with the intractable Martha.

He had shown he was adept at general practice and, looking around at new faces and old and listening to the vibrant chatter, it was apparent he had brought with him the new blood and fresh vigour without which the practice might never have survived the difficult transition into present-day health care.

She caught his eye suddenly over the heads of others.

His gaze held hers and she ached for the man she loved. She would never be able to tell him, of course. Life was never that simple. Martin's infidelity had hurt deeply, but it came nowhere near the intolerable emptiness she felt when she thought of life without Reece.

Just then Reece smiled at her, a smile that could only be for her, and her heart tightened in a sharp pang of pain and love. Now she could only be thankful to Martin that he had betrayed her for, had she gone through with the ceremony, hers would have been a loveless marriage. At least she had been spared that. Though would she have ever known what love was if she hadn't met the man with the sea-blue eyes, who was gazing at her across the room?

It was a dull, overcast Saturday early in March when Ben's memorial service at sea took place. The conditions had been too rough during February to attempt it and so the day finally dawned when the *Cancreel Maiden* set out for the open sea as a break in the weather appeared.

She was a stout, clinker-built vessel, smelling of marine paint and engine grease, and she bobbed buoyantly on the choppy swell beyond the harbour, the spot designated by Reece and the boat's owner as the appropriate area for the service. Her owner, Chas Miles, who usually chartered his boat to weekend fishermen, stopped the engines briefly as Reece recited a short fisherman's prayer and Holly cast the first of the beautiful floral tributes—from the Avis family—into the water.

Others followed—an anchor made up of blue and white blooms from the surgery, a heart of red roses from the home-care worker and sprays of early spring flowers from neighbours. The final wreath was a circular one of white roses and green laurel from Pullman and Fryer. It was accompanied by the ashes from the urn as Reece, dressed

warmly in yellow oilskins, began to intone the last prayer.
'Our Father…'

Holly reflected how Ben would have loved to have
planted his feet on the solid planks of this boat and breathed
in the salty air. He had known every mile of the Land's
End to Barnstaple coastline and he had once told her that,
after becoming housebound, he had still listened to the
shipping forecasts, from which he had derived his greatest
pleasure.

What might have seemed incomprehensible information
to some people, he explained, was the language which had
kept him alive over the last years of his life. This, then,
was his last journey and the most appropriate memorial, an
occasion made easier by the break in the bad weather which
allowed them to hold the service.

Very soon the engines started afresh and the boat picked
up the threads of her journey, turning towards harbour as
the waves lifted the craft's bow high in the water. With
Reece standing behind her, and dry in her oilskins, Holly
inhaled the wind and spray as the boat cut her way through
the waves. Soon the familiar coves came into view and the
cliffs and beaches she had walked so often slipped gently
down to the harbour mouth.

'Just in time, by the looks of it,' Chas shouted to them
as they chugged into calmer water and the rain tumbled
down from black skies. 'The weather's on the turn. We
might never have got out this afternoon.'

His words were emphasised by a squall, which rattled
against their waterproofs and caused them to hang onto the
rail. At last the *Cancreel Maiden* docked and the engines
were cut. Rain lashed decks and people alike. They said
their farewells to Chas, and Reece helped Holly make the
leap to the harbour steps.

It was a short five-minute drive to her house and, having
stripped off their wet gear in the hall, Holly took the oil-

skins to the utility room and hung them to dry. When she returned to the kitchen Reece was making tea and had placed the tray on the kitchen table, along with cups and saucers, side plates and forks. Raiding the cupboard, he had discovered a fruit cake.

She stood for a moment and watched him. His movements were easy and casual, the kind of motions that came from familiarity, from knowing where things were kept and returned to.

She allowed her eyes to linger on the white T-shirt, the thin material strained by the rounded, tight muscle beneath. His deep tan had lasted over the winter months in England and his black hair was now longer than it had ever been, softly touching the base of his neck. His long, athletic legs, encased in jeans, moved slowly over the floor and the memory came back to her of the first time she had ever seen him—dressed in the flying jacket, sitting with his legs sprawled out in Peter's rocking chair in the staffroom.

'Sugar...' came the preoccupied murmur, not to her but to himself as he opened first one cupboard and then the next, pausing as one did when looking directly at an object and not seeing it.

'Second shelf,' Holly said, unable to hide her smile as he turned and caught her looking at him. 'In the canister there.'

'Ah, right in front of my eyes.' He grinned, a boyish, lopsided grin, the same kind of smile that had charmed Martha and Josie and which, no doubt, had charmed so many other women—a thought which brought another anxious little pang to her heart.

'Reece—?'

'I thought perhaps we might eat out this evening. That is, unless you've something planned?' Still with his back to her, he poured water into the teapot.

'Reece, can we talk?'

He turned slowly, his blue gaze suddenly registering the urgent tone of her voice. He left what he was doing and came to take her in his arms. Laying her head on his chest, she closed her eyes. For a few moments he stroked her hair, then his hands ran down the soft checked cotton of her blouse and finally came to rest on her hips, his fingers slipping into the back pockets of her jeans as he prised her slowly away from him and looked into her eyes. 'Of course we can talk. Let's take the tray and sit down.'

Together they walked to the sitting room and as he lowered the tray to the coffee-table she sank on the sofa, watching his movements with a yearning that seemed to stretch all her emotion into a concentrated pain, untenable and isolated somewhere inside her.

He finally sat, his big hand reaching out for hers, and it was a few seconds before she began. 'It won't be long before you go,' she said, circling the rim of her cup with her index finger, 'and I wanted to explain about Martin.'

'There's no pressure on you to do that,' he said quietly.

She looked up at him. 'I know, but we've shared so much I wanted you to know the truth—why I called the wedding off. The truth was Martin had fallen in love with someone else. I happened to discover it by accident, seeing him and Sara out together one day. When I tackled Martin he didn't deny it, but explained it had been a short affair which was over.' Holly looked up and into Reece's frowning gaze.

'He said he loved me and he wanted to go on with our wedding. I agreed because I believed he really did love me—and I thought I loved him. Then I happened to bump into Sara one day. She was in a terrible state, having discovered she was pregnant. The child was Martin's and we were then just a month away from getting married.'

Reece shook his head slowly. 'But Brendan gave me the

impression it was you who called it off—in effect, that you jilted Martin.'

Holly nodded. 'I let everyone think that because Martin was in a difficult position. He was about to have promotion at work. As a solicitor with a small, select practice, his entering into a partnership hinged on our marriage and our settling in the town where we lived. It's a small community and Martin's deception wouldn't have gone down very well at all.'

'But how could he possibly let you take the responsibility?'

Holly leaned forward and set her cup on the table. Not meeting his gaze, she said, 'Because once I'd met Sara and knew she was expecting, I realised I had less to lose than Martin. He had started a family. And so, to save everyone embarrassment, I called off the wedding and almost immediately I applied for the post here in Cancreel.' She took a deep breath. 'Martin and Sara are married now and have a little boy. Everyone assumed he married Sara on the rebound and I've never told the truth to anyone but you.'

Reece gently pulled her into his arms. 'Oh, my poor, poor love,' he whispered.

'I didn't want you to think I was like Cassandra,' she admitted into his shoulder. 'I know she hurt you badly.'

He was silent for a moment, his breath coming shallowly, and her heart almost stopped in anticipation of his answer. Then he said, 'One man was never enough for Cass and she certainly wasn't cut out to be a doctor's wife. Her life was quite a social whirl in London and yet I had convinced myself she would settle down after we were married.

'Her father was a stockbroker and pretty horrified she had decided to go for a medical man, yet I think perhaps if I had chosen anywhere but Cancreel to return to she might have married me—which would have been a disaster, of course. When she finally realised the kind of life she

would be leading as a provincial GP's wife she knew it
wasn't for her.'

'But why did she let you down on your wedding day, of
all days?'

'Cold feet at the last moment, I suppose, combined with
one of her admirers showing up in Cancreel a couple of
days before. I think that rather decided it. Cass always did
have a sense of the dramatic.'

'And then you left for America?'

Reece gave a harsh laugh. 'Australia, Canada and then
America. I think I was trying to restore my damaged ego,
by keeping on the move. Eventually a colleague from university, who was already in Immediate Care on the East
Coast, asked me if I was interested. And you know the rest.'

Holly drew herself up and looked into his eyes. 'Do you
still think of Cass?'

He took her face between his hands. 'For the last six
months I've only had one thought in my head. And it hasn't
been of Cassandra.'

Holly felt the tears prick behind her eyes. They had never
realised how much they had had in common, yet perhaps
in some subconscious way they had because the attraction
between them was deeper than anything she could explain
in words. Her biggest regret was that she had never talked
to him about Martin before.

And now it was too late. At least she had set the record
straight and they could part without any secrets between
them, a thought which was too ironically painful to consider now.

She wanted to tell him she loved him. She wanted to curl
into his arms and tell him she had never felt this way in
her life before. Instead, as he drew her towards him and
whispered her name, his lips came down with urgent need
on hers and she let the moment pass, losing herself one
more blissful time in the world of make-believe.

CHAPTER TWELVE

By the middle of March Martha Macreedy was discharged from hospital and agreed, again with some persuasion from Reece, to go into Greenhills for a period of convalescence under the care of Don and Gill Miller. Jonathan Avis, within a few weeks of developing his new interest in computers, had taken a remarkable leap towards recovery. On this Monday morning Reece had asked Holly to meet him not at Jonathan's home on the estate but at the day centre which he attended twice a week.

The day centre, once a church hall, was now used for charity functions, and a section had been set aside for table tennis. Jonathan was playing when Reece and Holly walked in. Using a wheelchair similar to Jonathan's, a young disabled woman was his opponent and the competition between them was fierce.

Finally winning the game, Jonathan drew his arm across his forehead—an arm which had added muscle and strength over the weeks—and wheeled himself briskly to shake hands with his young partner.

At that point Jonathan saw them and waved, and Reece and Holly were introduced to Liz. 'Well done,' said Reece, smiling broadly. 'That's a damaging serve you have there, Liz.'

'Not damaging enough, unfortunately.' She laughed. She was a pretty girl, blonde and blue eyed and obviously fond of Jonathan. 'I'm waiting for the day when Jonathan lets down his guard and I'll finally be able to win.'

'You're doing pretty well yourself,' Holly said to Jonathan who looked nothing like the boy of last year who had been so devastated after the upset with Gary Sharpe. 'How's the computing coming along?'

'Fantastic!' cried Liz, and everyone laughed as she blushed.

'I met Liz,' Jonathan explained, coming to her rescue, 'through one of the home pages on the Internet. We discovered we have the same interests and, though Liz comes from Bude, we manage to meet at least twice a month and contact each other daily by E-mail.'

'And we're setting up a register for our area to help other disabled people link up,' Liz added. 'It looks as if it will be quite a full-time job as we are approaching other associations who might like to offer support.'

'We've already got a barbecue planned for the summer,' Jonathan said enthusiastically. 'Perhaps you'd both like to come?'

Reece glanced briefly at Holly before he answered. 'I'd like to, Jonathan, but I'm due to fly back to the States very soon. Sooner than I'd planned, actually.'

Holly realised she had sensed something different in his attitude as she'd walked into his consulting room this morning but before she'd had time to say anything he'd drawn her into his arms and held her close.

'I didn't expect it to be so soon,' Jonathan said in surprise.

'Nor did I.' Reece shrugged. 'A flight came up before Easter and our new partner is waiting to occupy her consulting room so I saw no reason not to accept it.'

'Well, this is goodbye, then.' Jonathan held out his hand. 'Thank you for everything you've done for me, Dr Caine, and for Mum and Dad, too. They seem to have taken on a new lease of life recently.'

'I'm glad it all worked out well, Jonathan.' Reece shook his hand firmly. 'Take care, won't you? And good luck to you and Liz with your new venture.'

After saying their farewells, Reece and Holly paused outside the church hall. The village was coming to life and a few early tourists were making their way around the little shops and down to the harbour. For a few moments Reece and Holly leaned silently against the church wall.

'I'm sorry you had to find out like that,' Reece murmured at last. 'I was waiting to tell you this evening, but when Jonathan mentioned the barbecue I hadn't much choice but to say something.'

Holly nodded slowly. 'When is the flight exactly?'

'A week tomorrow. The Tuesday before Easter.'

'A week,' she repeated numbly.

'I know it's soon, but it was either that or the week after. One of the guys from the aeromedical team is collecting me from JFK and, because of work commitments, he preferred the Tuesday so I accepted the booking.'

Holly had tried to imagine this moment and to prepare for it but nothing could have prepared her for the emptiness she was now feeling.

'Oh, darling, I'm sorry,' he sighed. Reading her thoughts, he reached out and took her hand.

She swallowed back the tears. 'We both knew this had to come, that when you went back to the States it would be over, and we both agreed it was what we wanted. Don't worry. I'm all right. It was just a bit of a shock, that's all.'

She managed a smile and looked at him, wondering how she was going to survive the rest of the day. She simply couldn't collapse into a heap. And she had enough pride not to burst into tears. So she squeezed his hand and took a deep breath of the soft spring air so her aching heart was again hidden, a heart which would have to mend despite the feeling she was consumed by—that life had no meaning at all without him.

The next shock came on Friday when, after morning surgery, Peter asked everyone for five minutes of their time in the staffroom. As virtually all the staff were in, the little room was crowded, with just Jo left in Reception to handle the telephone and any callers.

Celia Morton was there, too, for she had already begun to familiarise herself with the running of the practice and had shared several surgeries with Reece. Now the four doctors sat next to the reception staff and Alison, Joy and Holly occupied the chairs by the window.

Peter stood by the desk, brushing back his light brown hair and clearing his throat. The room fell into silence as a small smile touched his mouth for a few seconds.

'We have three rather unique events happening within the next month or so,' he began. 'The first is a sad one for Marge and I. Reece will be leaving us next week to return to his aeromedical team in America. We shall miss him more than we can say. If it hadn't been for his efforts and support over the past six months I'm sure we should never have seen the light of day this year.'

A general murmuring of assent trickled through the room and Holly felt her throat tighten. She dared not catch Reece's eye and, sitting back in her chair, she concentrated on Peter's face.

'The next event is more cheerful. We would like to extend a welcome to Celia, who will be our new resident partner after Easter. Welcome, Celia, from all of us.'

Celia responded with a warm smile, then Peter looked across the seated heads to where the receptionists and Judith sat. 'The final matter is entirely a personal one,' he said hesitantly, 'but we decided we should like you all to share in our happiness. Judith and I are going to be married.'

An astonished silence filled the room and then there was an almost deafening noise as everyone clapped and threw in their astonished congratulations.

'It sounds rather old-fashioned,' he went on with a wry smile, 'but it was a case of love at first sight. I had thought the chance of finding someone like Judith had passed me by. Heaven knows why, but she accepted my proposal only three months after we first met. That's why we've wasted no time—which brings me to my last point. I've decided to semi-retire and Judith is going to work in conjunction with Bronwyn, whom we hope will eventually take over as practice manager.'

Holly glanced at Bronwyn who was blushing deeply. Everyone clapped once more, the decision obviously well received.

'All that's left for me to do is to invite everyone present to our wedding, which we have arranged for May fifteenth. Invitations will be going out, but Judith and I hope you'll all be able to come.'

Then, as Peter and Judith occupied all the attention and were surrounded by well-wishers, Reece walked quietly over to where Holly was standing by the window. He looked down at her and smiled, reaching out to draw his fingers briefly over her arm. She could not help wishing that the happiness Judith and Peter had found had spilled over to them. For a moment she allowed the fantasy to develop until reality finally returned and she was left with the terrible despair which was, inevitably, the result of her self-inflicted torture.

Finally, Jo hurried into the room and explained that a representative from a pharmaceutical company had arrived. Reece left with her, his final glance making Holly wonder once again how she was going to exist without him.

Holly left the room a few moments later, after offering her congratulations to Peter and Judith. She managed to keep her composure until she reached the Fiesta and then the weight of what was happening seemed to impinge. The world was happily going about its business, but the sense of apprehension which had been her constant companion for months was now a blanket of pain and despair.

Much as she wished Peter and Judith all the happiness in the world, her own despondency deepened, intensified by the couple's delight in finding one another and the prospect of a future together. She drove to the cliff-top car park, locked the Fiesta and climbed the steps, remembering how she had felt last time she had been here when Reece had stood beside her, awaiting the helicopter.

There would always be memories now. Wherever she went, whatever she did, Reece would always be there. As she gazed across the ocean to the distant horizon she allowed the tears to fall. At least no one could observe her here and something about the constancy of nature, its strength and depth and colour, helped to ease the ache inside.

Holly chose to work on the day of Reece's departure. Their parting the day before had been painful enough, and to have travelled with him by train to Heathrow would only have prolonged the process. Saying their last farewells had taken all the strength she'd had and the day passed in numb grief and loneliness, though she worked without stopping and hoped that the exterior she effected was good enough to convince most people she was her usual self.

In the following days she had tried to fill every hour, every minute. At Easter, reluctant to stay in the house, much to her mother's delight she visited Cumbria, driving up on Friday and staying at the hotel until Monday. The following weekend she travelled to Looe to see an old schoolfriend and the weekend after that she spent gardening, filling her small garden with bedding plants and seeding the lawn where the winter frosts had browned the grass.

At work there were new patients from Dr Napier's surgery which had now been taken over by a younger man, allowing Dr Napier to retire. Celia Morton had placed three new post-operative cases with her and, as Peter and Judith were making preparations for the wedding, there was a general air of excitement, all of which seemed far removed from Holly's own detached world.

No matter what she did she thought of Reece. Sometimes she caught herself staring at the phone and wondering why he had never contacted her, and although she was tempted and had an address she knew she would never write.

The only news she had of him was through Marge and Peter, and that was limited. He had apparently transferred to another team and was now in Florida. Holly spent hours trying to imagine what he was doing and where he was, and even caught herself listening to or reading the news from the other side of the Atlantic.

Martha Macreedy moved permanently into Greenhills from the sheltered housing and had come to terms with her lot. Josie was doing fine at her new school and had not had a relapse. Ken Filler was also stabilised on his medication, and Jonathan continued to improve both physically and mentally. But if Holly saw less of the patients with whom she affectionately associated the brief six months in her life which she would never forget, new patients came along to fill her busy lists.

Then one day Holly realised that seven weeks had passed since Reece had left. It would soon be Judith and Peter's wedding. The ceremony was to take place in Durnweston registry office and Peter and Judith, who had surprised everyone with their romance, had settled, just as romantically, on a fortnight's honeymoon in the Caribbean.

The fifteenth arrived, warm and balmy—unusual for May. Hawthorn blossom spread over the country hedgerows and wild hyacinth appeared in little clusters of colour. The gulls circled even more noisily for the tourists' crumbs and there was a permanent mist in the early mornings, hinting at the rise in temperature.

The couple were to be married at ten and the reception, at Chartwell, was scheduled for twelve. Holly had decided to opt out on the registry office ceremony. Although she had been invited she felt the service was probably more appropriate for close family.

Therefore she dressed leisurely, deciding on a silky, powder-blue midi-length dress with a tiny waist and dainty straps. The simple waist-hugging jacket in navy blue—the colour that always reminded her of Reece—she complemented with classic navy low-heeled shoes and linked small pearl earrings. Her freckles had reappeared with the sun and her hair, the longest it had ever been bounced glossily around her shoulders, shedding its chestnut light each time she moved.

Just as she was about to leave, the phone rang. She hesitated about answering it but did, unable to ignore its call. She was surprised to hear Bronwyn's voice.

'I've arrived at Chartwell,' Bronwyn explained in a flustered fashion, 'and I've stupidly forgotten my wedding gift. I left it in Reception under the desk. As I knew you were driving out later I hoped I'd catch you before you left. Would you mind bringing it with you, Holly? There's no Saturday surgery this week but the cleaner will be there to let you in.'

'Of course not, Bronwyn. I'll see you soon.' Holly made sure she slipped her own gift of silver cutlery into the car and, glancing around the house for the last time, closed her front door and locked it.

Saturday morning surgery was usually under way but this morning had been set aside for the celebrations and Dr Napier's young locum had offered to take the on-call until that evening, when Celia would take over.

Holly was surprised when she entered the surgery. The

cleaner was nowhere to be seen and the place seemed deserted. Going to the desk, she searched for Bronwyn's gift but it wasn't there. Nor was it in the office or in any of the other rooms, though Holly made a thorough search in all of them in case someone had moved it. Now she was worried. Had someone taken it while the cleaner was occupied?

Deciding to look upstairs in the cloakrooms and staffroom, she made a quick tour of the ladies' loo and then, her steps quickening, pushed open the door to the staffroom.

It was deserted. There was nothing even faintly resembling the gift—a large box containing glassware and wrapped in decorative paper, Bronwyn had explained. Nevertheless, Holly opened all the cupboards and drawers and when she had finished stood, frowning, in the middle of the floor.

The only solution she could think of was to ring Bronwyn at Chartwell. Going to the pay phone, she took several coins from her bag, lifted the receiver and dialled. Holly began to feel apprehensive. No cleaner and no wedding gift and, now, no one answering at Chartwell.

'I think this is where I came in,' said a deep voice behind her, 'but this time I don't intend to behave quite as badly as I did before.'

Holly spun around. Her reaction was one of complete disbelief. She gazed incredulously at the long jeans-covered legs and above them the deep blue eyes fringed by heavy black lashes and filled with an expression which made her heart stand still.

'Perhaps try again later?' Reece said, grinning. 'After all, they're probably enjoying themselves too much to worry about the phone, don't you think?'

Holly returned the receiver to the hook, her hands shaking.

'Say something,' he murmured, slowly rising to his feet.

The sight of his tall, wonderfully familiar figure filled her with a sudden completeness, as though his presence had brought her back to life from a deep, deep sleep.

Before she knew it she was in his arms and kissing him until she could hardly breathe, her heart racing behind her ribs. 'Oh, Reece,' she gasped, holding his face between her hands, as though he might disappear, 'you're supposed to be in America, aren't you?'

'I was—but none of it made sense any more. Not without you.'

'But you didn't write or phone—'

'What could I have said? That I missed you and this place and the people in it and the six months which brought me the greatest happiness of my life? What sort of a response would I have got, I wonder, from such an independent lady, who seemed so happy and content with her life before I came on the scene? No, I had to look straight into her beautiful soft grey eyes before I said it and see her reaction for myself.'

Then he kissed her again, more slowly this time, searching for her response. She gave it, moving against his body with aching familiarity. 'I love you,' she whispered as she gazed up at him. 'I love you so.'

'Then why didn't you tell me before I left?'

'How could I? You had another life to return to—commitments with the team, responsibility to the work you loved and, for all I knew, a relationship with someone else.'

He held her firmly away from him and drew his brows together in an angry frown. 'Do you really think that? After all we meant to one another?'

Holly shook her head. 'I didn't know what to think—'

'Holly, don't you know I've been head over heels in love with you from the first moment I saw you? But you told me you were content with our temporary arrangement, though I kept hoping you'd try to convince me otherwise.'

He took a deep, shuddering breath and held her close. 'When I landed at JFK I knew America was a part of my life that was over. I had found the place I wanted to be and the woman I wanted to be with. But I didn't know if you felt the same. Even changing to an aeromedical team in Florida couldn't stop me thinking of you night and day. All I wanted to do was come home.'

She shook her head, still unable to believe what he was telling her. 'Do you mean home—here, in Cancreel?'

'I mean home with you.' His eyes were full of amusement. 'And if I'm lucky I might get my old job back. Peter said he's hoping to semi-retire so there will be room for someone else eventually.'

Holly sank against him and closed her eyes against his cotton shirt as she inhaled the scent which was so uniquely Reece. Then she looked up and frowned. 'There never *was* a wedding gift, was there?'

'As soon as I arrived this morning I rang Chartwell and Bronwyn answered the phone. We cooked up this little subterfuge between us.'

'And I suppose if Bronwyn knows…?'

'Everyone knows.'

She laughed softly and stood on tiptoe. She placed her lips softly on his, pushed her hands into his hair, pressed her hips against him and sighed. 'And I take it there's no cleaner either?'

He shook his head, pulled off her jacket and bent to kiss the smooth, bare skin of her shoulder. 'No cleaner. No one. Just us.'

'Then we've still time,' she whispered wickedly as she began to undo the buttons of his shirt, 'for a little immediate care.'

MILLS & BOON®

Medical Romance™

COMING NEXT MONTH

'Twas The Night Before Christmas...

CAROL'S CHRISTMAS by Margaret Barker

Carol needed to talk to her husband, Euan, the new Casualty consultant. Did he *really* want the divorce to go through?

INSTANT FATHER CHRISTMAS by Josie Metcalfe

Midwife Livvy was so busy, she missed the signs of her own labour! Perhaps it had something to do with the unexpected arrival of her estranged husband, Daniel.

ONE MAGICAL KISS by Helen Shelton

Will persuaded Maggie to give him just one Christmas Eve kiss to put an end to his attempts to seduce her. But what a kiss!

MIRACLES AND MARRIAGE by Meredith Webber

Emma was wary. It was hard to take Patrick seriously in his Father Christmas outfit but when he kept mentioning marriage, it was even harder.

Available at most branches of WH Smith, Tesco, Asda, Martins, Borders and all good paperback bookshops

CHRISTMAS

Affairs

MORE THAN JUST KISSES UNDER THE MISTLETOE...

Enjoy three sparkling seasonal romances by your
favourite authors from

MILLS & BOON®
Presents™

HELEN BIANCHIN
For Anique, the season of goodwill has become...
The Seduction Season

SANDRA MARTON
Can Santa weave a spot of Christmas magic for Nick
and Holly in... *A Miracle on Christmas Eve?*

SHARON KENDRICK
Will Aleck and Clemmie have a... *Yuletide Reunion?*

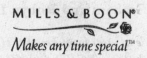

MILLS & BOON®

Makes any time special™

Available from 6th November 1998

Your Special Christmas Gift

Three romance novels from Mills & Boon® to
unwind with at your leisure—
and a luxurious Le Jardin bath gelée to pamper
you and gently wash your cares away.

for just £5.99

Featuring
Carole Mortimer—Married by Christmas
Betty Neels—A Winter Love Story
Jo Leigh—One Wicked Night

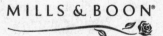

MILLS & BOON®

Makes your Christmas time special

Available from 23rd October 1998

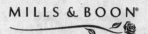

MILLS & BOON®

*M*akes
any time
special

Enjoy a romantic novel from
Mills & Boon®

Presents™ Enchanted™ Temptation

Historical Romance™ Medical Romance™